SALEM'S GHOSTS

By M.C. VAUGHN

SPLINTERED INFINITY PRESS, LLC.

SAVANNAH, GA., USA.

Acknowledgements:

First of all, many thanks to my family and friends for their continued support and encouragement.

As always, extra-special thanks to Danny Simanjaya for his ever-wonderful cover art. Danny can be found on DeviantArt as Simonjova. I hope we will be collaborating again on the next of these novels – soon!

Thanks also to Chris and Angela, Steve and Sheri, Josh, Jaimie, Gideon and Pat. Shoutout also to the crew at Experience Poker – especially Robin for his endless patience in dealing with the nonstop shenanigans. I hope there's a poker room on the other side, where we can play, laugh and cuss at each other without end.

In memory of Jerry Greene. I wish you were still here to read this.

For my Dad. Whether you like it or not.

SALEM'S GHOSTS

IN MEMORIAM

From the McDowell Mills Herald:

SMITH, FREDERICK STEVEN – born August 16, 1932, Tuckerton, Ga; entered into eternal rest on Wednesday, March 14, 1993, at his home outside McDowell Mills. Mr. Smith was a Korean War veteran and longtime resident of our town. He is survived by one brother, Andrew Harris Smith, Tuckerton, Ga.; sister-in-law Carolyn Smith, and nephew Steven Smith, also of Tuckerton, Ga., along with several more distant cousins. Service date and location to be announced. In lieu of flowers, the family asks that donations be made to the USO.

CHAPTER ONE

I MOVED TO MCDOWELL Mills with my parents in the spring of 1993, almost thirty years ago now. I had lived my entire life in the suburbs north of Atlanta, where people were usually somewhat educated and relatively sane, and I knew going in that leaving Tuckerton would be an unpleasant shock. I would be leaving my friends and my school behind for what was still mostly farm country, and I wasn't happy about it at all. And still, I wasn't ready for what was coming.

The reason for our move was the death of my uncle Fred, who had owned a farm not far outside town, and who had been an idiot and a total jerk for as long as I could remember. During the previous winter, he had been diagnosed with pancreatic cancer, and it killed him faster even than the doctors had expected it would.

In death he had proven to be even worse than in life, where he had treated our whole family with rude disdain: he left our more distant relatives his money, which had not been inconsiderable, and left my dad his farm. Dad was pretty hacked off about that. After the three of us realized that we would have to manage the place ourselves until we could sell it off, we all were.

Fred didn't leave anything to his own family because he didn't have one. My guess was that any woman who spent more than ten minutes around Fred realized that there wasn't enough money in the world to make it worth putting up with him. More than once, when my dad and I disagreed on something, my mom made a point of reminding me that I should be thankful that my dad wasn't more like him. Uncle Fred was so obnoxious that her admonitions usually got the results she clearly wanted.

I remember telling my friends in Tuckerton where we were moving, and receiving mostly blank looks in return; McDowell Mills was a name most of them had at least heard before, but where none of them had ever been. Well, almost none of them.

"Be sure you tell your dad not to speed," my best friend, Jim, warned me one afternoon as we were walking home from school. That was another thing about the move that sucked: in Tuckerton, I lived a block from the high school, and could get there and back in five minutes. The mall was less than a half mile away. There were plenty of places to go and things to do, even for the bunch of bored teenagers that we were. McDowell Mills, from an entertainment standpoint, was a wasteland by comparison.

"We know about the cops down there," I answered him glumly. And we did know. A semi-evolved sheriff's deputy with a voluminous beer gut had pulled over my father – with the entire family in the car – just inside the McDowell Mills city limits for the capital offense of doing forty-one miles per hour in a zone where the limit was thirty-five. Instead of writing my dad a ticket, like any civilized police officer working for a real department would have done, that deputy called for backup, arrested him, stuffed him in the back of his police car, and took him two miles from there to the county jail. We had had to come up with a hundred and fifty bucks to bail him out, and he had emerged from the experience none too impressed with local law enforcement.

"And the girls. You'll want to come up here on the weekends," Jim had added. Again, his observation was entirely too astute; seeing a beauty salon in the town square sporting a garish sign that proclaimed "JOLENE'S GREAT BIG HAIR" made me realize that I was entering a sort of time warp, travelling between ten and twenty years back as measured by the social clock. I don't know whether the place was so backward that it took that many extra years for light to arrive ("they have to pipe in sunlight down there," Jim had also sagely mentioned to me) or if it was because most of the locals were so dense that their collective presence literally curved space/time. From a good-taste standpoint, I strongly suspected the latter.

But eventually, every last piece fell into place, completing the really crummy puzzle that was my immediate future. Our house in Tuckerton sold quickly, and I had to pack all my stuff up over a single Friday evening. Dad rented a box truck and the three of us handled the move, making multiple trips starting Saturday at dawn. We left my mother at Fred's house after the first trip, once we saw how bad the living conditions were. Fred could fix anything, so all the appliances worked and the house was structurally sound, but he hadn't seen the point in cleaning or dusting anything. At all. Ever. Mom was horrified at the state of the place. She wasn't alone in that, either.

I had protested the move to my parents, offering to drive back and forth to Tuckerton for school each day. That gambit had proven about as effective as most teenage resistance; after being scoffed at by my dad for proposing to drive almost eighty miles a day just to go to school, I was informed that I would definitely be attending the local high school instead.

"The school there isn't as good as Tuckerton. You're going to have to make even better grades there than you've been making, if you want to get into college," my mom had said. At least she left it at that; she knew I wasn't happy about going to a worse school. I know now that on some level, she was no more pleased than I was – not that that mattered. She was right, and later, after my first ten minutes spent observing some of the lunks who populated that institution, I could confirm that she was right. "And you won't be able to get a job until after the farm is sold," she added. "Your dad and I can't keep it up alone."

She had been right about that, too. Dad was still working at the airport as an aircraft mechanic; for him, his commute was barely longer than it had been before. But Uncle Fred had had his own way of doing literally everything, and without him there, it took three of us just to figure out what needed doing, and do it. At least Dad managed to sell Fred's cattle off almost immediately. I think we'd have been overwhelmed if we'd had to deal with them along with everything else. I don't think he got much for them, but then, I wouldn't be surprised if he paid someone to come get them. I probably would have. The situation was that bad.

So finally, on Sunday, April 11, 1993, we finished moving in. I will never forget that day – it was fourteen hours of uniquely teenage bitterness and anger at the enormous amount of work that had to be done, as well as the reason for it all. By the time it was more or less finished, the house was almost clean enough for my mom to live in, we were all gross with the grime that had coated everything, and I had to get up for school the next day. And no, I didn't get to drive there.

"You need to practice driving Fred's truck for a while before you get out on the roads around here," my dad had said. I knew how to drive my mom's Toyota – which had a four-cylinder engine with an automatic transmission – and in my ignorance, I had figured that that would be sufficient experience. At least, that's what I thought until I actually got behind the wheel of the truck. It was a 1971 Dodge D100, beat all the way to Hades and most of the way back. It was rusted half through, the interior was nastier than the house had been, and the transmission was manual – a three-on-a-tree. I stared in dismay at the column shifter for about two minutes while my dad laughed at me. Jerk.

I don't really mean that. I just thought it at the time.

RIDING A SCHOOL BUS at age sixteen is a bit like dating someone who picks their nose: you might get used to it after a while, if you have to, but it's just not pleasant. No one ever lets you forget it, once they've seen you doing it in public. It gives people who otherwise have no business making fun of you license to do just that. And you'll take any other option available the moment it presents itself.

I was the only driving-age person on that elderly Blue Bird vehicle on my first day at my new school, other than the driver herself, and she had more in common with the other passengers than with me. If I hadn't already guessed that, I would have known at once from the unanimously contemptuous sneers that greeted me as I boarded.

It was seven miles from Fred's farm – I absolutely refused to think of it as home – to the county high school in what passed for downtown McDowell Mills. The drive took twenty minutes and felt at least twice that long. I sat in the third row, well away from most of the riders in the back, and far enough behind our surly-looking driver that she wouldn't be able to hit me with the juice from her noticeable wad of tobacco even if she tried. Or so I hoped.

When the bus pulled into the lane at the school to let us out, I got a taste of what a new prison inmate must feel on arriving to begin their sentence. Clumps of T-shirt-and-jeans rednecks who could have answered the casting call for "Grease" en masse – assuming they could read – were scattered on the sidewalks and in front of the building. The contempt for me that had radiated from the other riders receded into the background as a sort of angry sullenness took over their mood. They had all been through it before, and were used to what to expect. I think on some level, they all had calculated that my presence would overshadow theirs, and that they could at least hope to be less noticeable.

I went down the steps onto the sidewalk with my head lowered and made for the building with as much casual quickness as I could muster, not looking at anyone. I could feel stares following me, but as long as I didn't actually meet any of them, I could at least try to convince myself that they weren't real. Fortunately, the entrance was close enough that I was inside the building before any taunting could start.

The school's front office was relatively quiet; a middle-aged, bespectacled secretary sat behind a desk wall that hit me just above the waist. She looked supremely bored.

"Good morning," I said. She looked up at me from a book she was reading, gazed at me with an empty expression, and waited for me to say something that would prompt her to an actual response.   It was a bit unnerving, how lifeless she looked.

"I'm Steve Smith. I just moved here, and I came to pick up my class schedule," I continued, trying not to feel like I was talking to a corpse.

I don't know how she did it, but somehow, she made her dead face sag. "What year are you?" she asked in a dull monotone that further reinforced the entire image she projected.

"Junior," I replied, trying not to sound bitter. It was another reminder that I might well have to graduate from that place, and already I wasn't happy about it.

She got up from her chair as slowly as I already expected she would, and made her way to a filing cabinet that stood in a corner behind her chair, walking slightly hunched over. I'm sure she knew exactly which drawer to look in, but she still moved her index finger along the labels on the top two drawers before opening the third one. That same slow finger moved glacially backward along the drawer's contents until pausing for at least five seconds. She then drew a single sheet of paper out of a file folder that clearly had been added recently, studied it absently, and then peered at me. "Steven James Smith?" she asked.

"Yes, that's me," I responded. She gave the ghost of a snort in reply.

"There's already five Steve Smiths here. Guess nothing would do except to add another one," she grumbled, much more to herself than to me, as she ambled back to her seat and held out the sheet containing my locker assignment and schedule to me, addressing me more directly: "I assume you can read this."

I didn't know it at the time, but then, I hadn't met the football team yet, so I didn't realize that that was an actual concern. I nodded as I looked over the page's contents, then glanced toward her to find that she had already picked up her book again. Sighing, I folded the paper and pocketed it, looking for room 407 and my first-period American Literature class.

GOING TO A NEW school involves being uncomfortable most of the time, including some ways that no one ever mentions. One of those uneasy moments reared its head as I entered Mrs. Oldendahl's Lit class just as the bell rang, and realized that there were no available desks.

She looked over at me. She seemed pleasant enough; she was a nondescript, fortyish woman who was – I know no better way to describe it – dressed like the teacher she was. She frowned slightly when she saw me enter, but not in an unfriendly way.

"Mr. Smith?" she asked.

"Yes. Steve," I replied.

"Mr. Smith," she said again. I expected to see a response from the class, but either Mrs. Oldendahl had great classroom management, or she had drugged them: no one so much as blinked. "I had requested another desk be added in here, but as you can see –" she waved her hand vaguely toward her silent students – "it has not arrived. I'll need you to sit on the floor under the window today."

I nodded and started toward the spot she had indicated. I had just sat down, feeling very out of place and visible, when I realized she had followed me, and was handing me a copy of Steinbeck's "Of Mice and Men," along with a decent-sized, generic-looking Literature textbook.

"Thank you," I said unnecessarily as I took them; she didn't respond, and after a few moments, she was in front of the class again. Most of the students seemed to be asleep, but a few were paying close attention, and after about a minute of listening to Mrs. Oldendahl, I understood why. She was the kind of teacher who, without resorting to excessive outbursts or attention-getting behavior, could present material like Steinbeck's – who, like most high-school students, I found rather dull – in a way that made it interesting enough to make me consider actually reading it.

But what struck me most about her was this: she didn't give two hoots whether anyone listened or not. She knew full well that most of her students were paying her no attention whatsoever, and instead of trying to browbeat them, she simply taught whoever would listen and allowed the others to suffer the inevitable consequences of their lassitude. She did glance over at me once, about five minutes in – I'll bet she could tell within five minutes of starting each semester which of her students would succeed and which ones would fail – and a tiny smile tugged at the corner of her mouth when she saw me still awake and attentive.

My first hour at MMHS passed more quickly than I expected it would. I wasn't alone in that, either – when the bell rang to dismiss us, I heard at least four separate yawns and more than a few waking groans. I had already stood up to leave when

I noticed that two of the more alert students were watching me. One was an obvious nerd, but not of the helpless variety; he looked like he had some common sense. The girl beside him was short, a little heavyset, and shared his street-smart demeanor. I had noticed both of them paying rapt attention to Mrs. Oldendahl earlier. Neither one seemed unfriendly, so as everyone else filed out of the room, I decided to approach them.

"Steve?" the nerd asked. I nodded.

"Chad Campbell," he continued. "This is Stephanie Johnson," he added, motioning toward the girl, who smiled at me with a weird mix of uncertainty and frank speculation. Not being sure of how to respond, I nodded to her, and heard myself say, "my next class is Analytic Algebra and Trigonometry. Where's room 208?"

"Just come with us," Chad answered. "If you're in Oldendahl's class, and you got through her lecture without snoring, then you're probably tracked with us. We're going to AAT, too."

I didn't have a lot of choice in the matter, since I didn't know the building layout, so I followed them as they left the classroom and began picking their way through the crowded hallway beyond.

One thing I learned from my mercifully short time in McDowell Mills was this: you can tell how good, or bad, any school is by looking closely at the best students in it. Are they social outcasts? Do they show signs of stress or dysfunction? It's probably not a very good school, if academic achievement is accompanied by social ostracism. I've never seen a more prime example of this phenomenon than in MMHS.

Chad and Stephanie were two genuinely kind, intelligent, conscientious students, socially awkward and a little bit sheltered. In Tuckerton, they would have been surrounded by an entire community of teenagers just like them, and would have functioned perfectly well. Unfortunately for them, their birth lottery ticket was a loser: McDowell Mills, both as a school and a community, glorified athletics, popularity and conformity to the exclusion of almost everything else.

This misalignment of priorities was evident as we made our way through the halls to second period AAT. My new acquaintances were used to generally disdainful treatment; if anyone had recognized me from the bus, their malice went unnoticed by the pair. None of us spoke, and I wondered whether they were already regretting having invited me along with them.

When we arrived at room 208, I breathed a sigh of relief; the average run of students all had to take – and, unless they were athletes, pass – American Lit in order to graduate. For that reason, teachers like Oldendahl were forced to deal with pretty much the entire student body. AAT, on the other hand, was well past the level of math required for graduation, which meant that no one took it unless they were actually serious about academics.

Unfortunately, that also meant that a certain amount of leeway was given to the instructor, and Mr. Singer used every inch of it. And not always in a good way. Singer was short, bald, and loud. When his attention fell on you, you knew it at once, and on a clear day, half the county did as well.

"Steven Smith! You here?" he asked, loudly, looking around the class as though he couldn't see me. At least he, like

Oldendahl, was up to date on who was in his class, and unlike first period, there had been several empty seats available. I raised my hand. "Stand up so we can get a look at you," he blared, pointing at me. Every head in the room turned.

Gritting my teeth and thanking whatever god had been assigned to small-town high schools that only the math nerds were seeing this, I rose from my empty front-row desk, red-faced with the embarrassment reserved specially for teenagers subjected to unexpected, undesired, undivided attention. I could feel twenty-two pairs of eyes on me.

"Tell us where you came from, Mr. Smith," he continued, in his best crowd-control voice. I knew I couldn't get away with outright refusal, and scorched-earth resistance might reap unwanted results, so I rolled my eyes very slightly and scowled.

"I used to live in Tuckerton," I answered unwillingly.

"Tuckerton!" Singer boomed. "They have lots of farms in Tuckerton? Feed stores on every corner? Free bait with every gas fill-up?"

"No, sir," I replied. Mistake.

"Sir? No SIR? Don't tell me they teach *respect* in Tuckerton?" came the loud response.

Exasperated, I risked a glance back. Stephanie was on the row next to mine, three seats back; she looked both impressed and sympathetic.

Thankfully, Mr. Singer waved me off as I was about to speak. "OK, that's enough. You've been properly introduced." Unsure as to exactly what sort of impression I had made on him, and red-faced from the unwanted attention, I retook my seat with alloyed relief.

We turned out to be studying base mathematics. My school back home had already covered that more than a year earlier, so I glanced over the problems in the book while listening to Mr. Singer. I didn't see anything that I couldn't solve.

I don't know how long he had been watching me as he taught. When I looked up to the front again, he was still speaking, but he clearly had seen my attention drift.

"I suppose they don't teach respect up north of town after all," he commented, looking directly toward me, with a smile that was both mirthless and somehow conspiratorial. It was so puzzling that all I could answer was, "I'm sorry, I was just checking the material in the book."

"You've already been over this, haven't you?" he asked in reply. This time he looked serious, but I still couldn't be sure he wasn't just jerking my chain.

"Yes, sir," I replied. I was spared another barrage about respect, mercifully.

He turned to the board and wrote out a fairly simple base-conversion problem, and then came over and handed the chalk to me. "Show us how you would solve this," he said.

I wasn't thrilled to be called to the front, but at least I absolutely knew I could answer his question, so I took the chalk and walked to the blackboard.

"First thing I would do is convert each term to a common base," I said, rewriting the equation in base ten. "Then I would solve the equation, and then convert the answer back to the base you requested." As I wrote on the board, my glance shifted between the chalk, Mr. Singer, and the class; I could see that about half of them looked slightly confused, but the rest –

including Chad and Stephanie – were obviously appraising me as I worked.

All at once, my opinion of Singer significantly improved: I realized, looking at my classmates, why he had put me through that little charade. He nodded to me as I handed him the chalk and returned to my desk. Chad also nodded, and Stephanie smiled a little. A couple more approving looks were cast toward me as I sat down and refocused on the lesson.

The rest of the period passed quickly enough, and as the bell rang and everyone gathered their stuff to leave, I looked back at Chad. "I have Chemistry next," I said.

"Chem, then U.S. History, right?" he asked in reply.

"Yeah." I was already set to leave, thinking that I would only be following two people. Instead, I realized that most of the right side of the room was waiting for me.

I looked from face to face, meeting each gaze in turn. It felt weirdly like an initiation – which, as it turned out, it was, though I didn't know it at the time.

Before I could respond, the entire group started moving out of the room. I left in their midst; Chad was ahead of me, and Stephanie behind. Chad waited in the hall until I was alongside him.

"I think you've been accepted," he said.

"That's nice, but to what?" I asked. Stephanie had caught up to us and was next to me on my right.

"It's kind of a weird story. Do you believe in ghosts?" she asked.

At the time, I was a raging agnostic. I was willing to believe that supernatural stuff was possible, but I'd never seen anything like that that was even remotely convincing. By the time I was in middle school, I was pretty sure it was all a load of bunk.

"Not really," I answered, trying not to be rude about it. After all, I didn't have anyone else offering to be even remotely friendly with me. And she was sort of cute. Sort of. At least, that's what I thought at the time.

"A lot of us didn't," Chad said on my other side. I looked over at him, trying to figure out whether he was messing with me, but it didn't seem that way. He looked as unsure as I felt. It took me a second to figure out why.

"Should I?" I asked. If they were going to try to lead me on some sort of high-school snipe hunt, I couldn't see any real harm in that. At least from their crowd, anyway. If they had been the football team or the guys in the auto-shop classes, I wouldn't even have considered it.

"Depends. You want to hang out with us?" he answered.

My heart sank at double speed. "Until I figure out how to drive my uncle's truck, I'm stuck riding the bus," I answered. "And even then, I have to help keep his farm going until my dad can unload it."

Chad's eyebrows went up. "Wait. You're Fred Smith's nephew?" he asked.

"How did you know?" I asked. Stephanie snickered audibly. Chad was grinning.

"Did you like him?" he queried, clearly watching me for my response. I glared at him.

"He was the biggest jerk I ever met in my life," I said. Stephanie's snickers turned to outright laughter, and Chad joined in. I had no idea of how to react. Fortunately, we had reached the Chemistry classroom.   Chad went in, still chuckling, but Stephanie clutched at my arm.

"We aren't messing with you. I promise," she said. I thought that either she was a really good actress, or she thought it was really important that I believed her. I smiled a little, still more than slightly confused by the turns my first day had already taken, and went into the next class, hoping that Chemistry would be no harder than AAT had been.

CHAPTER TWO

BY THE END OF MY first week at MMHS, I had learned a lot more about my Uncle Fred, and why my distaste for him amused my new friends so much. Fred had, one way or another, scammed almost everyone over thirty in McDowell Mills that wasn't directly connected to what passed for the local aristocracy, and was no more popular there than he had been in my immediate family.

Several of the people in my new group – including Stephanie – had parents who had come off worst in their dealings with him, to the point that over the last ten years of his life, no one in the county would do business with him. Not that he cared; the farm was lucrative enough for Fred to support himself without dipping into his savings, and as a general rule, he hated dealing with people anyway. He did, however, ensure that he paid his taxes religiously, donated to the right local political candidates, retained the most prominent local attorney, and generally maintained the connections he needed to insulate himself against any complaint brought against him by most of the town's actual population.

So, my friends fully comprehended my dislike for my dead uncle, though I took a certain amount of ribbing for having such an unfortunate relative – as if I'd ever have chosen him. Still, they actually *were* my friends. Chad had turned out to be the captain of the academic team. There wasn't a study-related club at the school that didn't have him or Stephanie as a member. Most of their circle of friends were in the same groups, and they all pretty much welcomed me as one of them. I appreciated that, since it hadn't taken long for me to realize that aside from the brain trust, there was no social group there that would have fit me. Even the real zeroes wouldn't have welcomed a bus rider. I guess they probably got enough abuse from the jerkier factions at school without that.

On Friday afternoon, Stephanie met me outside my Business Composition class – the only one she didn't have with me – and invited me to hang out with their friends that night.

"Can't," I replied. "I haven't figured out my uncle's truck yet." And I hadn't. I'd gotten about thirty minutes' practice with it during the week, and the thing had already demonstrated to me that it was the perfect vehicle for my uncle: it was as intractable, obnoxious and prickly as he was, with seemingly no redeeming features. Even worse, it smelled like him – hand-rolled cigarettes and stale beer, mostly; no doubt Fred had also been generous in his donations to the sheriff's office – and I knew that fixing it up would be a dirty, all-weekend job.

"We'll pick you up," she answered.

I considered. "I was kind of wondering what you guys do around here," I finally answered. "Where I come from, there's a lot of different places to go, but here, it's…" My thought trailed off.

"Boring," Stephanie finished for me. "The only things to do are the movie theater and bowling alley over in Jackson

Creek, but no one goes there. The greasers run the bowling alley and the theater manager is a jerk – he always runs us out."

"Sounds about like everything else down here," I grumbled.

"Exactly," she said. "Then they wonder why so many of the younger people are leaving. The smart ones all know there's nothing here for them, so each generation, the people who are left get dumber, and there's less of them." She paused. "Everyone in our crowd is planning on leaving as soon as they get to college. I'll bet you want to move back to Tuckerton, too – don't you?"

"Yeah." I thought about that for a second. "Not that I don't like you guys, but I *really* don't belong here."

"None of us do," she answered. "The greasers and the jocks who don't get scholarships are the ones who'll get stuck here, since they're too dumb to go to college. Anyone smart enough to go on after high school is smart enough to get out of here."

I nodded, shrugging. "So what did you guys have in mind?"

She smiled again, but that smile had an I've-got-a-secret quality to it that was both intriguing and unsettling. "Has anyone told you that this is the most haunted town in Georgia?"

My mom and dad had actually talked about that over dinner earlier in the week. "I heard something about that. My parents think Savannah is probably more haunted. But I told you, I don't believe in ghosts," I replied, as Chad came up behind Stephanie. He gave me a funny look.

"You don't have ghosts in Tuckerton?" he asked loudly, sounding remarkably like Mr. Singer. Stephanie laughed a little at that. I frowned.

"There's places that people say are haunted, but I've never seen anything. I always thought they were just something people made up to scare anyone stupid enough to believe in them." This was certainly true. I'd been in a graveyard on Halloween, and once I spent the night with some friends in an abandoned house that was supposedly the site of a murder, but the only thing that I ever had to deal with was the swarms of bugs in the house.

"Well, here it's different," Chad answered. He glanced about, and his voice lowered as he continued, "there's five or six places that people say are haunted – the civil war cemetery, the place where the train wreck happened, the burned church out near where you live – but there's one place that no one talks about, and it's not like the others. The people in town will say there's ghosts in those other places and then try to milk the stories as much as they can, to make money. Our place is outside town, and it's *really* haunted."

"And the other places aren't?" I asked. I liked my new friends, but at the same time, I wasn't completely one of them – at least not yet – and the last thing I wanted was to have my chain jerked.

"We haven't seen anything at any of those other places," Stephanie replied. "Believe me, we've looked."

"After we found out about where we're going tonight, we went to the others to see if they were there, too," Chad added. "There wasn't anything. Not in any of them, not ever. But this one place –" Chad grinned again, shaking his head. "It's *weird,* dude. It's not even scary. But there's *definitely* ghosts there. A *lot* of them."

I thought about that for a moment. I could have stayed home, but McDowell Mills was still waiting for its first cable TV service offering, and it was so far out from Atlanta that the television display was mostly static. Dad was planning to install a big antenna on the house over the weekend, but that wouldn't happen until Saturday afternoon, at the earliest. It would be a dull night if I didn't go.

"Where is it?" I asked. Dullness wasn't enticing, but I still preferred that to anything that involved breaking even minor laws, given how the local police usually behaved.

"There's a public park that borders the graveyard for the First New Jerusalem Methodist Church," Chad answered. "We go and set up chairs near the fence, and just hang out, starting around sunset. They're a lot easier to see after it starts getting dark. Most of them don't pay any attention to us, but there's a few that come over and talk, at least sometimes." His smile faded a bit, and Stephanie nodded. "The park doesn't close until ten, so we usually just get burgers and eat there, and wait."

At that point, even if they were just messing with me, I had already decided I would go. If I was being pranked, so be it. They were still the only friends I had.

It never occurred to me to wonder whether there was really anything to what they said, or whether there really might be ghosts there.

FOR DECADES, THE good-old-boy network in McDowell Mills had resisted the march of chain stores across the

American landscape, choosing instead to protect the mom-and-pop businesses that had existed there for generations. It was all part of the chokehold that a select few families held over the politics and economics of the entire county, as well as its professional, educational, social and even religious communities. Cross the wrong people in McDowell Mills, and you might as well leave.

As a result, the only burger joint in town was an old diner – Cleve's – just off the main square that looked like it had come out of an advertisement from about 1955, and hadn't been painted or remodeled since then. It was clean enough, and the takeout food wasn't any worse than you'd get at a drive-through chain, but there wasn't anything better for miles around, and there wasn't going to be anytime soon.

The three of us rode in Chad's nondescript but serviceable truck – the sort of vehicle most males in the town drove – north on Highway 255 to the edge of town as the afternoon deepened into sunset. About three miles beyond where the last residential streets ended and the surrounding farmland began, a large Methodist church – the First New Jerusalem Methodist Church – had been erected at the intersection of the highway and New Salem Road.

"They built it here after the First Methodist in McDowell Mills split, about sixty years ago," Chad said. "The congregation that split off didn't want to be called the Second Methodist Church. They thought they should be first, so they moved outside the town limits, built their church there, and named it for the road."

I could only shake my head. "Sounds about right," I said. "From what I've seen, you can't tell the church people around here anything. They already know it all." I'd already been approached by several of the church youth-types at school; those conversations had been brutally short. Rather than waste time stringing along their hopes with noncommittal responses, I ended them as quickly and bluntly as possible. This had become known as a "mercy killing" among my new circle of friends, and had been a source of considerable amusement for them.

"Exactly," Stephanie laughed in reply. "Until it comes to actually living their beliefs. Then it's all 'judge your neighbor' and casting stones and all that garbage."

"Stephanie!" Chad admonished her. She jutted her chin at him and answered, "well, that's what it is!"

Chad sighed, and we finished the rest of the short drive in silence. Fortunately, New Jerusalem Park was only about two miles ahead, and another truck was waiting for us when we pulled in and parked near the fence on its back end. Beyond lay a cemetery that, while not new, was nowhere near as old as some of the churchyards in town. Most of the stones were unreadable – not from time, but because we were looking at them from behind.

About five hundred feet beyond the fence, Highway 255 continued north toward Atlanta, and the church's sanctuary and steeple reared beyond that. The graveyard continued on the far side, to the left of the church, and those headstones appeared even at that distance to be somewhat older and more ornate than the stone sentinels and metal, ground-set plates nearest to us.

I looked over the cemetery as Stephanie slid across the driver's seat, carrying our takeout bags, and exited behind Chad. It seemed bigger than I would have expected from a church that was, by county standards, relatively new – especially one that had started with a split – but then I remembered that our food was getting cold, and at any rate, I really didn't expect to see anything that night other than my new circle of friends, so I let it go at that.

Chad had already pulled three lawn chairs out of the truck. He had remembered to bring one for me, which I greatly appreciated since I hadn't known whether I'd need one. We set them up in front of the truck, a few feet back from the fence. Three other chairs were set up in front of the other truck; I recognized their occupants as members of the academic team, but I hadn't learned their names yet. When Stephanie handed out our food, I discovered with some dismay that the fries had gone a bit limp. I ate them as quickly as I could while she talked.

"They usually start showing up right around sundown," she observed. "I don't think we've ever seen one in full daylight, but sometimes if it's cloudy, we can see them during the day."

"I did," said one of the other watchers. He sat in the middle chair in his group, and was skinny with a blond buzzcut that emphatically didn't suit him. "But it was only once, and just for a couple of seconds."

"Really?" Stephanie asked him interestedly.

"Yeah. Couple of months ago." He paused. "This the new guy?"

"Steve Smith," I said, unnecessarily. He nodded in reply.

"I remember you from Singer's class. I'm Joey Ray," he said.

I couldn't resist my next question. "Is Ray your last name, or your middle name?"

"Ha ha," he answered, clearly not put out by the query. "It's my last name. My parents aren't Neanderthals."

"Good," I answered through my last handful of fries, reaching for my wrapped burger. It was still warm. Chad looked over his shoulder toward the sunset.

It's almost time," he said.

I had not forgotten that we were supposedly there to see ghosts, but I also fully expected some sort of prank, so as casually as I could, I glanced around at my surroundings. There was no one else in sight, and no hiding place where someone could lurk in wait anywhere within a hundred yards, except maybe behind some of the larger markers. If this was a setup, it was coming from the people waiting with me. The shadows lengthened as the sun slid below the treeline, then disappeared.

"There," Stephanie whispered, pointing. I followed the direction of her arm, and almost choked on my last bite of my burger.

There was a middle-aged man, maybe forty-five, standing in front of us about fifty yards away, looking toward the church. He was brown-haired, and wore formal clothes that had probably been in style right after the Second World War. He had just appeared in that spot out of nowhere.

"It's Mr. Abbott," Joey said.

What I was seeing was unbelievable enough as it was. "You know their names?" I asked, completely taken aback by the remark.

"Yeah," the girl next to him replied. I remembered her name was Lori, or Laurie; we hadn't talked before. "When we first found out about this place, we mapped out all the gravestones, and then did research to try to match pictures of people with the ghosts." She pointed to the apparition, which looked unnervingly solid – not like I would have expected – and was already walking away, then thumbed through a notebook in her lap. "Albert Abbott was killed in a house fire in 1957." She closed the notebook. "There were rumors that his wife started the fire, but there's no reason to believe that – at least, there's no proof. He never talks to us, though, so we can't be sure."

"Is his wife here? Maybe we could ask her," I couldn't help saying.

The girl gave me an odd look. "His wife left McDowell Mills before the grave was filled in. Never came back. Who knows? Maybe she did do it. There's a lot of stories like that here."

Even as she spoke, several more ghosts literally appeared from thin air among the gravestones and standing flower urns. I actually saw one woman who looked to be about fifty, dressed in clothes of similar vintage to Abbott's, materialize where there had been nothing an instant earlier.

I looked toward the others. "Either this is real, or your technology club is the best in the state. Maybe the country."

"They're real," Chad answered. "But not everyone can see them. We don't know why. Most of the people at school can't. Some of the jocks used to make fun of us, until one day they showed up out here and started trying to make us leave. Pastor Samuels actually came out of the church after them, and man, they sure could see *him.* They all probably wet themselves as they ran off."

"Who's Pastor Samuels?" I asked.

"He was the minister at the church until about ten years ago, when he finally died. He had to have been at least eighty. But one of the jocks was his grandson, and recognized him, and I know for sure *he* wet his pants when Pastor Samuels started yelling at them to leave." Joey's grin was shared by the rest of the group. "Can't blame him, either. The ghosts can be scary when they get mad, but that doesn't happen much, and they never get angry with us for just watching them."

I thought about that for a moment. A few more figures materialized, and I realized as the evening began to fade that they were still as bright and visible as if lit by daylight.

"So most of them just walk over to the church?" I asked Chad.

"Yeah," he replied. "For most of them, I think their idea of heaven is going to church every day. I don't know if they realize they're actually dead."

I thought about that. It sounded absolutely terrible – getting up and going to church literally every day, for eternity.

"Have you ever talked to any of them?" I finally asked.

"There's a few that sometimes come over and say hello," the girl beside Joey said. "They kind of seem like they're not thrilled with going to church."

"Your name's Laurie, right?" I asked her.

"Lori," she corrected me, emphasizing the long 'O' in her name.

"Sorry," I answered. "But I think it's funny that it's the misfits who don't want anything to do with what everyone else is doing – they're the ones who come talk to you guys."

"Birds of a feather," Stephanie answered. Then she drew in her breath sharply and pointed, with a big smile on her face. "Look! It's Tommy!"

Another ghost – this one about nine years old, from his appearance – had trotted toward us. The image of a ghost trotting – even a ghost child – was the oddest thing I'd seen yet. He stopped near the fence, looking at us inquisitively, and asked, "Have you seen my ball?"

"No, sweetie, we haven't," Stephanie answered.   The boy's face fell.

"I have to go in to church now. I hope I can find it when we get out," he said, and trotted away more slowly, looking disappointed. I was stunned to see tears forming in Stephanie's eyes.

"His name was Tommy Barton," she said thickly. "He got run over on the highway there, right in front of the church. The story was that he was chasing after a ball." She gulped and shook her head, and continued more steadily, "He died about ten years ago – I remember when it happened." She bent her head for a moment as Chad put his arm around her. "He was a good kid."

"Does he always ask about his ball?" I asked.

"Always," Chad answered, looking very bummed. "Most of the time, the same people do the same things, day after day. There's a few that only appear once in a while, but not many."

"If it's always the same, why do you hang out here?" I asked.

"To see if something different happens. There's one ghost especially that we're hoping to see," Joey said. "She almost never appears, and when she does, she just comes over and looks at us. We don't know why. Usually it only happens when we bring someone new, so we thought we'd bring you."

"We're not sure who she is," Stephanie said. "We think she's about our age, and she died around 1950, but she's not buried here. Or if she is, she doesn't have a marker."

I thought about that for a while. "Have you ever tried telling any of them what happened to them?" I asked.

"I did, a couple of times," Joey said. "They just ignore what you say. It's like they can't hear you when you try to tell them. I tried to tell Tommy, more than once, but he just wandered off."

Across the cemetery, I could see more of the ghosts wandering toward the church. On the highway's far side, I could see ghosts in the other graveyard, and even at that distance, they looked like they were acting strangely. Looking over at Chad, I asked, "What's going on with them?"

Joey started laughing, and the others joined in. "You can't see it from here, but one time, I acted like my truck had broken down there so I could get a closer look," Joey said. "The ghosts on the other side of the highway act like it's *their* church, and that the people on this side are just newcomers who need to mind their place. They get pretty loud about it, too."

"Wait. Aren't they all in the same church?" I asked.

"Not it hear them tell it," Chad said. "The older churchyard is closest to the sanctuary, so they're the old-time members. You know how it works. The people who have been around longest think they get to decide everything. That's why this church split in the first place. So the newer members argue a lot with the old members, but after a while, everyone goes in the church, and that's usually it for the night."

"Wow," I said. "I'm still trying to figure out how anyone could think that's heaven."

"I think it's all they know," Lori put in.

Even as Chad had described it, the ghosts had massed near the church, and were either dematerializing into it, or vanishing altogether. "And you have no idea why we can see them and no one else can?"

Chad shrugged. "No clue."

After another minute, when the last apparitions had winked out, we were packing our chairs and preparing to leave when Stephanie said, in a low voice, "Oh, my God. There she is."

I looked up. A girl like they had described was walking through the cemetery toward the fence. It was almost full night, yet she appeared bright as day. She moved slowly, and as she approached us, I realized that she looked faintly desperate, as though she were in some slight pain that never went away.

The others all stopped as she drew closer, watching her. She came all the way up to the fence and looked at each of us, one at a time, until she got to me – and her expression changed.

Her mouth fell open as she saw me, before her hands rose to cover it. Her eyes were round, and she seemed to breathe in a gasp – if ghosts could breathe, that is. Her hands drew forward across her lips until they were palms together, as though she were praying. I think now that she might have been doing just that.

"Oh, my God," Stephanie breathed again.

The girl looked at me, and I stared back at her, for what seemed like minutes. She had been very pretty, and was wearing a white sundress that I guessed was from the early fifties. She bit her lip as she looked at me, as though she would burst into tears, before whispering, "Freddy?"

My blood ran cold. I knew that my Uncle Fred and I had shared a family resemblance – another of his many qualities that I detested – but evidently, when he had been my age, the resemblance had been even more marked. Whoever this girl was, she had known my uncle, and not casually.

I felt a hand on my arm. "Come on," Chad said, half dragging me to the door of his truck. I couldn't take my eyes off her. He almost had to lift me into the seat before my eye contact with her broke; Stephanie had already climbed in, and the others were already starting to back out of the parking area. I looked at her again. She was still watching me, and as we started to pull out, my blood ran cold again.

"Oh, man, she's *following* us," Chad hissed, and he was not mistaken. She was moving no faster than a human girl would, but she had gone right through the fence and was walking behind us as we turned to leave the park.

"Wait!" I said, but no one listened. I glanced back as we pulled out onto New Salem Road, and saw that she was still following us. Chad gunned the motor, heading south toward Tin Roof Road, and the trees obscured her.

Neither Chad nor Stephanie spoke. We passed Tin Roof and went uphill, back toward McDowell Mills, until I finally said, "guys. Let's pull over for a minute."

Chad looked at me for a long second, then nodded, and slowed the truck as he eased it onto the shoulder and put it in park. Both of them were looking at me.

"She doesn't know who I really am, so she can't follow us any farther than the first fork in the road without getting lost," I said.

Stephanie looked at me. "She called you 'Freddy.' Why would she think you were your uncle?" she demanded.

I shrugged. "I don't know. At least, I don't know how she knew him. But I think I'll have to find out. Something's wrong with her. She wasn't like the others at all."

"I just thought she didn't like church," Chad said. "But man, did she lock onto you."

"I know," I said glumly. I felt drained, and overwhelmed. "I just wish I knew why. She looked like she's been waiting a long time for something that isn't coming."

"Maybe it *is* coming," Stephanie said. Chad and I both stared at her.

"She has to have some connection to your uncle. She never really paid attention to any of us after our first visits," she continued. "And she *definitely* didn't react like *that*. I just wish I knew why."

"I could ask my dad," I said shakily, still glancing into the side-view mirror from time to time. There was no sign of the girl.

"Do that," Chad said. "And see if there's anything in the stuff he left, if you haven't thrown it away. It's like Stephanie said – she looks like she died around 1950, from her dress and her hair. We checked through the local paper, more than once, but we've never seen anything about her at all – at least, nothing that we could connect to her."

"Maybe she wasn't from McDowell Mills," I ventured.

"Then why is she in the New Jerusalem graveyard?" Stephanie asked, a little too loudly. She was still rattled by what had happened. We all were.

"I don't know," I finally answered. "I'll try to find out. But I don't understand why you took off like that. If you were so interested in her, why'd you peel out the minute you had a chance to find out more about her?"

"She didn't scare you?" Chad asked. "She sure scared me." Stephanie nodded in agreement.

"No," I replied. "I just felt terrible for her. I felt like she needs something, really badly, and that she thought I could help her." I swallowed. "I *want* to help her, if I can."

For that, they had no answer.

CHAPTER THREE

"WHY ARE YOU ASKING all these questions about your Uncle Fred?" my father asked. My mom was in Fred's old galley kitchen, putting the last touches on supper. The burger and fries hadn't been particularly good, and I was still hungry when Chad and Stephanie dropped me off.

"That's the first thing people asked me about at school," I said. "People wanted to know if I liked him."

Mom came to the table with a bowl of mashed potatoes and a plate of pork chops, setting them down next to the broccoli and gravy she had already prepared. "I don't think *anyone* liked Fred," she remarked, as she sat down. "He was a lot older than your dad, so they weren't close."

She was right about that, too, and I had been worried that would be the case. Dad was born in 1949, when Fred was seventeen, and was still an infant when Fred joined the Army and went to Korea two years later. When he returned home, he moved out the next day, and within a week he had used what he had saved from his military salary to buy the farm we now lived on. Dad had said more than once that Fred had probably made a lot of extra money fleecing the other GI's at cards, but I wasn't so sure about that – at least not from the price of the farm.

"Do you really think he had that much money when he came home?" I asked.

"He only paid $50 an acre for 30 acres, and he was making over a hundred dollars a month," he replied. "Even with the buildings and equipment, he wouldn't have needed to borrow money, and as far I know, he never trusted banks, but he still had more money than he should have."

"When did he tell you all this?" I asked, spooning potatoes onto my plate.

"He didn't," Mom broke in. "I went through some of his paperwork when I was clearing out his desk. I found the bill of sale for the farm, along with his old pay stubs and a lot of other stuff."

I thought about that for a while. "What about the attic? Has anyone been up there yet?"

"No," my father replied, emphatically. "That attic is probably full of every nasty bug on earth. I was going to set off a bug bomb up there tomorrow."

I was relieved to hear that, until Dad said, "I'll set it off tomorrow first thing, and then we can go up to Jonesboro and get some more cleaning materials. I know for a fact that there's a ton of stuff up there, so we'll need masks and gloves to clean it all out."

That didn't sound like a lot of fun, but I figured that at least I'd get a chance to look through everything, so I just nodded and kept eating.

"After we get that cleaned out, you and I can start working on you driving that truck," Dad added.

That sounded a lot more inviting, so I nodded again, more enthusiastically, as I chewed a bite of pork chop. "Thanks," I mumbled.

"Don't talk with your mouth full," Mom admonished me.

BRIGHT AND EARLY the next day, Dad and I laid out painters' drop cloths over the entire lower story of the house, and then the three of us piled into his SUV and headed off to the big hardware chain-store in Jonesboro. It would be almost a forty-minute drive all told; thankfully, Dad planned a stop at a pancake house on the way.

Some four hours later, after we'd picked up enough lumber, nails and paint to redo most of the front porch, along with plenty of cleaning materials for the stuff in the attic, we headed back to McDowell Mills. Dad had insisted on wedging everything into the SUV, and it was uncomfortable, but there was nothing else for it.

"If you have anything hanging out your back window, the local cops'll ticket you for it," Dad said. "If you put a red flag on it like you're supposed to, they'll just tear it off." This had actually happened to an acquaintance of his that lived outside town. It was just another reason that everyone in the family wanted out of that place as quickly as possible.

It was almost two in the afternoon by the time we got back, unloaded the car, and got rid of all the drop cloths. It took Dad and me another hour to climb up into the attic and haul down everything that had been in there. Mostly it was just boxes of random stuff, but there were a few oddities, like a very old saddle that barely fit through the crawlspace door.

My dad gave me an odd look as I started to dig through the boxes. "I thought you'd want to practice with that truck."

I hesitated. If mom found anything about the girl at the park and didn't know it for what it was, she might throw it out. On the other hand, Dad knew I wanted to master that truck as soon as I could, and if I suddenly acted like the boxes were more important – whether they were or not – he'd want to know why.

"That's right," I replied. I looked at Mom. "Do you want me to get these when we come back?"

Mom looked relieved. "Sure," she answered. "I've already got to make sure all that bug spray is out of the kitchen. That'll be one less thing."

"Okay," I said. Dad was already over near the truck, on the driver's side; I figured he was going to drive us someplace like a parking lot, where it would be safer for me to practice. I climbed into the passenger side and looked around for a seatbelt, and then groaned. Dad was already trying to dig the buckle out from behind the seat on his side. I started doing the same.

"Gross," I muttered. I don't know whether Fred ever cleaned that truck out while he had it, but he definitely didn't take care of any detailing. It was like reaching under your seat in an old movie theater. God only knew how many old coffee spills had accumulated under there. Even when I finally located the buckle and started trying to unearth it, it was so slippery and gooey that I could barely pinch my fingers hard enough together to keep it from slipping out.

Dad had already gotten his buckle out. His expression of distaste matched mine. After a moment of glancing around the cab for anything that might make the thing less nasty, he got back out and went inside, returning with some damp paper towels. He handed some to me, and then started scrubbing the gunk off the buckle on his side.

After about five minutes of that, the seatbelts were usable, though still not very nice. Dad looked over at me as he started the truck.

"You want to start cleaning this up when we get back, instead of getting those boxes cleared out?" he asked me.

"Wellll...." I thought quickly. "I promised Mom that I'd do them, and anyway, it'll probably take me all day tomorrow to get this bucket cleaned up right."

He nodded as we backed out of our driveway onto the narrow road. As he drove, my dad showed me how to shift into each gear, and to clutch fully with each shift, easing off as he nudged the gas. It didn't look too hard, until we got into town and he pulled into the parking lot for the only strip mall in McDowell Mills, about a mile south of the town square. He parked at the back of the half-full lot, shut off the engine, and looked over at me. "Go on around," he said, unbuckling his seat belt and sliding across the truck's bench seat as I got out and went around the front of the truck to the driver's side.

When I had buckled back in, I checked the shifter to ensure that it was in neutral before cranking the engine. Dad gave me an approving nod, and I carefully slid the beast into first gear.

Immediately I understood why he wanted me to practice in a parking lot. The truck bucked once or twice, backfired like a rifle shot, and stalled. My dad started snickering as every head in the lot turned in our general direction.

"Damn it," I grumbled.

"Language, son," he admonished me, snickering harder.

I dropped it back into neutral, cranked it again, and shifted into gear a second time, being much more careful to feather the gas. It still protested, but not nearly as much, and I was actually able to get it going enough to shift into second before it did the same thing again.

At this point, several people were clustered around the grocery store door, and the other shops at the strip mall likewise were emptying out to watch my struggle. Red-faced, willing myself not to get frustrated, I tried yet again.

It took about twenty minutes of going back and forth across the end of the parking lot before I was finally able to complete a round-trip without at least one interruption. When at last I wheeled the truck back around toward the grocery store successfully, the crowd that had assembled outside the various shops to watch the festivities – I guess there must have been a hundred people in all – cheered loudly enough for me to hear them over the truck's engine. I was not encouraged.

"All right, son. Now go out the side of the parking lot and head back to the house," Dad instructed me.

I was finally getting the hang of the infernal vehicle, and sensing when to gas it, when to shift – and more importantly, when not to do either. The shifting order was a little odd – bottom, top, bottom – but I knew I'd get used to it. If I could get the old bucket cleaned up, it might actually be a decent truck. At least I knew beyond any doubt that when we moved back to Tuckerton, no one in their right mind would try to steal it.

THERE WERE STILL TWO hours of daylight left when we got back to the farm. I had successfully driven the truck all the way without any more fits or stalls, and my dad agreed that I would be ready to drive it on Monday. The relief I felt at not having to ride the bus any longer was even greater than I had expected it to be, but that could wait. I needed to attack those boxes on the front porch as quickly as I could.

I made a show of going inside and cleaning up before going back out to start working. I liked my Mom and Dad, and overall I trusted them, but for some reason, I wasn't ready yet to say anything about the girl – or any of the ghosts – to them. I also didn't want Mom to throw out something that might have been important without knowing it, and I *really* didn't want to have to pick through the trash if she did. That would definitely have prompted some uncomfortable questions.

I got a big trash bag and started with the first box. It turned out to be filled entirely with old bills from the sixties – power bills and phone bills, mostly. Fred had a well somewhere on his property, but had been hooked up to the county water system by the time he died. There were also some old invoices he had copied from work he had done for different people around the county. The earliest bill was from 1962, and the last was from 1969; when the box was emptied, with literally all of its contents going straight in the trash bag, I noticed that Fred had labeled the bottom of the box "1962 – 1969."

That was Uncle Fred – only he would label a box on the bottom, where only he would look for it.

Grumbling to myself, I turned over the next box, considered the label – "1970 – 1976" – and decided it could wait. I then checked the other boxes until I found one that looked as though it had been recently repacked, and whose contents spanned from 1950 to 1956.

I considered for a few minutes, and then opened it. At once I understood why Fred had repacked this one: all of his correspondence with the Veterans' Administration was in there, along with some other military-related mail, some really old bills, and – to my amazement – a series of receipts from a florist in McDowell Mills, starting in 1953 after he returned from Korea and continuing uninterrupted, the same day each month, until 1977. Obviously, he had written the dates on the box before he repacked it.

I couldn't *prove* that the receipts were connected to the girl, but knowing Fred, I couldn't imagine them being for anything else, so I set them aside. The rest of the box contained nothing more enlightening than the first one had, so I dumped out its contents, carefully folding and pocketing the florist's bills.

The afternoon waned past sunset as I dug through box after box, but nothing else seemed even remotely important to my search. By the time I finished the last one, filling my third garbage bag and finding nothing else of any value to anyone, I was ready to be done, but I knew there was something I was missing.

It was full dark by the time I dragged the trash bags to the huge can – at least this part of the county had garbage pickup; I had been horrified to discover that some of the more rural parts of the population had to take their trash to the landfill themselves – and broke down the dozen or so boxes I had reviewed. Going back inside, I washed up quickly, and then decided to have one more look upstairs.

The attic was lit by a single, dangling light bulb with a pull switch, and was only about as large as a small bedroom. The residual smell from the bug bomb was overpowering, but I was glad we had used it – literally dozens of creatures of every description, including a pair of small scorpions and at least three black widow spiders – had left their earthly forms behind in plain sight. I swept the corpses around me aside with my shoe and looked around, but the space was empty.

The floor was composed of rough wooden slats. I began examining each, trying to see whether any of them might be loose, until I came upon one with a long spider leg sticking out from a crack. Naturally, that board turned out to be looser than the others.

Hoping that whatever lurked on the other side of that board was indeed dead – that leg looked to be over an inch long – I worked my fingers into another small gap and tried to pull the slat loose. It came up surprisingly easily, and I breathed a huge sigh of relief when it came up. The wolf spider that had been beneath it was indeed dead, and had been even larger than I had realized. The knowledge that I had been sharing a residence with that monster was unsettling, but I felt better remembering that in all likelihood, it and all its buddies were either dead, or fled from the premises.

More importantly, a gray shoebox had been tucked between the ceiling joists underneath the slat. I blew away the spider – which had fallen onto the box lid – and carefully lifted it out from its resting place. It apparently had not been moved in a very long time; small ramparts of dust had slowly accumulated around its bottom edge, and the whole thing was grungy.

I was about to open it, but then remembered – Mom was making dinner, which would be ready any minute. I needed to get this box from the attic to my bedroom as fast as possible. I gave it a quick check for any stray surviving bugs, brushed the dust away as fast as I could, pulled the chain to kill the attic light, and scrambled down the ladder as quickly and quietly as I could.

Only a few seconds later, the box was on my dresser, and I was looking at it, preparing myself to lift the lid, when my mother's voice sounded dimly from the kitchen: "Steven! Time for supper!"

Trying not to act impatient – after all, the box would still be there when I was done – I pulled out the wad of florist's receipts from my pocket and laid them on top of the box, and then went to the bathroom to wash up for dinner.

TWENTY MINUTES LATER, I was back in my bedroom, staring again at the box lid, wanting to open it, but starting to worry about what I would find.

I didn't want to admit it, but the girl scared me. No one else in the whole crummy county had known me a week ago, but she had recognized the family resemblance at once. I figured she had to be buried there, somewhere in the cemetery.

If this girl had somehow had a relationship with Fred, and had died, that would explain a lot. It would explain why he bought flowers every month for all those years – perhaps he had been putting them on her gravestone, though it didn't explain why he had abruptly stopped buying them in the seventies.

Still, Chad and Stephanie didn't know who she was, and that struck me as really odd. They knew most of the ghosts that they had interacted with, but nothing about her. It didn't make sense – they should have been able to find her death date like the others they'd tracked down.

The only thing I could think of was that maybe her grave was hidden, or overgrown. I was sure my friends didn't know which part of the cemetery she was buried in, or exactly when she died, so it would have been hard for them to figure out who she was.

I took a deep breath, and carefully removed the lid. Inside, I found a batch of old letters strung together with twine, some old bills and receipts, a small box that looked like a jewelry box, and some old black-and-white photographs that immediately knocked the breath out of me. It was her, all right – but instead of looking pained, she was smiling brightly, and she was *gorgeous*.

After the initial shock of how pretty she was, the first thing that popped into my mind was – how in the world did a girl like her end up involved with my Uncle Fred? It just didn't compute at all. I couldn't imagine a girl that beautiful even looking twice at a guy whose truck and house were as nasty as Fred's were, let alone his equally nasty temperament. Still, the florist's receipts argued that at some point, Fred must have been more human than he was by the time I knew him.

I had to find a box cutter in my drawer to cut the twine on the letters. They were all postmarked from McDowell Mills, starting in mid-1949, and were all addressed to Fred, first at the family home near Tuckerton where he grew up, and then at the APO address for the Army, right up to the time when Fred got out of the service in 1953. There were no letters for him addressed to the farm.

So the girl had been from McDowell Mills, and had somehow met Fred in 1949, and had remained in touch with him until he returned from Korea – and then stopped. I guessed that that was about when she died. I thumbed briefly through the other photos; they were all of her, all smiling, all beautiful. I realized that I felt terribly sad, looking at her. She was barely older than me in the first ones, and she would be dead long before she would have even been twenty-five.

Beneath the photos and letters, I found a few newspaper clippings in the bottom of the box, and glanced over the headlines. Most of the stories were about a local hardware store, Beckwith's, that had apparently gotten closed down in the sixties by the GBI. From what I could gather from the stories, the owner had been mixed up in some sort of bootlegging or money-laundering operation, and had been sentenced to eighteen years in prison in 1965.

Eighteen years. That was a long sentence for money laundering, let alone bootlegging.

I went back through the photos again, looking on the backs for something that might give me a hint as to who this girl was, and on the last photo, beneath the words "May 1953," a neat hand had written delicately in cursive:

"For my Freddy. I can't wait for you to leave the Army and marry me. I love you. – Sarah"

My jaw dropped. Fred – *engaged* to this girl? I shook my head, but the thought wouldn't go away – at some point in his life, my uncle had been something other than the jerk he was by the time I was alive, enough so that a girl like this was ready to marry him.

Still, I now knew more about her than the others did. Her name was Sarah, and she had died sometime after May of 1953. She was from McDowell Mills, and probably graduated from the high school sometime around then, so she might have been in the school yearbooks. If this had been Tuckerton, it would have been much harder to track her down among the dozen or more high schools in that area – but there was only the one high school in the county. It had been rebuilt in the sixties, but I already knew some of the library books were older than that, so I could at least hope to track her down.

I looked once more at the letters. I knew that I couldn't ask my Dad about this; at the very least, I'd never see them again. There was no way I would ever tell them about the church or the ghosts, either – so if I was going to figure out what was going on, I was going to have to read them. All of them.

I grimaced. The thought of reading a love letter written to Uncle Fred was just… gross. Reading a whole collection of them was going to be a cringe-fest, but I had to do it, and since I was going to have to get the truck cleaned tomorrow, I needed to read them that night.

But then I remembered the look on the girl's – Sarah's – face, and realized that I might be the only one able to help her. I didn't care one bit about Uncle Fred, but she was different. I felt like she really mattered.

Sighing, and whispering an apology to her that I felt she probably wouldn't hear, I drew the first letter out of the slit on the side of the envelope and began to read.

CHAPTER FOUR

I GOT UP BEFORE eight on Sunday morning. My parents didn't go to church, which made things simpler for me, and I secretly hoped I could finish detailing the truck early enough to be able to meet Chad and Stephanie and go back to New Jerusalem.

The letters had told me much more about Fred and his relationship with Sarah – no surprise there – but it was really, really strange to read a woman expressing tenderness and affection for him, especially over and over again. Her gushing over kindnesses he had shown her or things he had said that pleased her were even more bizarre. If I had not known those letters were actually written to him, I would never have believed it. Ever.

I also understood some of why Fred kept that newspaper clipping. Sarah's full name was Sarah Grace Beckwith, and she had gone to the same high school I attended. She had dated him since her freshman year in school – he had been a senior – and had stayed in school while he went into the service. Somehow, she had fallen head over heels in love with him, and it looked like he had felt the same way about her – enough so that by the last few letters, she was already starting to plan their wedding once his service time ended. Her last letter even mentioned the very farm we had inherited, telling him that it was for sale and that her father was considering buying it.

As I emptied out the trash from the cab and the dashboard of the truck and began scrubbing the years of accumulated grime out, that last part kept coming back to me. Was her father going to buy the farm for her, or was he buying it for his bootlegging operation – assuming that he and the crook in the story were the same man?

Or was it both?

I mulled those questions for the next couple of hours, as gradually the truck's interior went from filthy to grimy to passable. The radio still worked – not that I wanted to listen to it; it was AM only, and it could only pick up the county's single radio station. Their music selection was apparently limited to country music recorded during the Truman administration, and really bad televangelists' recordings on Sundays. The blowhard's voice proclaiming out of the tinny speakers when I tested them reminded me that the first thing I would need to do, once the truck was usable, would be to figure out how to put a real sound system in there.

That last part kept me distracted while I cleaned out the well where the seatbelts had been. I was going to have to get new ones – the truck only had lap belts instead of the ones that went over the shoulder, and I wasn't real happy with them. Also, there were only two belts, so I wouldn't be able to take anyone in the middle seat unless I found a way to add another one. That was probably going to be expensive to fix, too.

It was past noon before I was finished with the interior of the truck. Dad had cleaned out the bed before we took it to town for me to make a fool of myself, but it was still nasty from years of hauling who-knows-what. After a few minutes' fiddling, I figured out how to lower the gate, and swept it out with a broom from the garage. We still hadn't cleaned that up yet. Dad and I would probably tackle that next weekend, and it was going to be bad – it looked much worse than the house had.

I was getting really hungry, and the truck was in good enough shape to drive once I washed it, so I went inside to get something to eat. It was already well past lunchtime. Dad was trying to watch the Hawks game on our TV – he had set up the antenna on the roof while I cleaned the truck – and Mom was fixing him a sandwich.

"You want one too?" she asked as I came into the kitchen.

"I'll make it," I answered. She smiled back in reply. I was about to open Fred's ancient fridge – Mom had restored it so well that it might have had some value as an antique – when the phone rang. Dad answered, and after a second, his voice floated into the kitchen: "Steve! It's for you."

Trying not to look like it was important – I knew it had to be Chad or Stephanie – I went into the den and took the receiver from my dad, and said, "hello?"

"Hey, it's Chad," came the voice on the other end. "You find out anything about the girl?"

"I think so," I answered. "You busy this afternoon?"

"Nope," he replied. "You got the truck ready?"

"Almost," I hedged. "I have to get new seatbelts for it, so only two people can ride in it, but other than that, it's good."

"OK. I'll get Stephanie and then come pick you up," he answered."

"You want me to just meet you there?" I asked, glancing toward my dad, who was studying the snowy TV screen, trying to follow the action in the game.

"We were going to the library," Chad replied. "They keep a morgue of the County Herald on microfilm, so if her obituary was published, we can find out more."

"Great idea," I answered, and glanced toward my dad again. "Dad, I'm going to meet a couple of friends at the library. I'll be back for supper."

"OK, son," my dad replied, still focused on the TV.

"See you there. Twenty minutes?" I said into the phone.

"That's fine," Chad answered.

"OK, see you then. Bye," I said, and hung up. I went back into the kitchen to throw a sandwich together, and discovered that Mom had already made one for me.

"Eat this before you go," she said, looking carefully at me. "I don't want you trying to drive that thing and eat at the same time."

I grimaced, not so much at her concern as from embarrassment at my first experience with the truck, but I did as she asked, once more trying not to look too rushed. Four minutes later, I mumbled a "Thanks, Mom," as I headed out of the house.

"Be careful!" she called after me, and I waved in response without looking back.

FIFTEEN MINUTES LATER, I pulled into the McDowell Mills Public Library parking lot, and eased my truck into a space next to Chad's. His cab was empty, so I killed the engine – thankfully, it chose not to backfire – and got out, and went inside.

The library was a low-roofed octagon on the street that became the same state highway the New Jerusalem church straddled, some five miles farther north. It was one of the rare places in town that was open on Sunday, didn't serve lunch, and wasn't a church. I supposed that was to allow students to use it for research over the weekends, but on this particular Sunday, my friends and I had the place pretty much to ourselves.

There were two microfilm viewers set up along one edge of the eight-sided interior, and Chad and Stephanie were waiting there for me. Both looked up expectantly as I approached.

"So – what'd you find out?" Stephanie asked immediately.

"A lot," I answered.

"Did your dad know who she was?" Chad asked. I gave him a funny look.

"Do you really think I told my dad about the cemetery?" I asked back. "I went up in our attic and cleaned it out. And you're welcome, because it was *really* gross up there. Anyway, I know who she is, I know about when she died, and I'm pretty sure she's buried at New Jerusalem."

"What's her name?" Stephanie asked immediately. I was a bit surprised by the intensity in her face, and I looked around quickly to make sure there wasn't anyone eavesdropping, and quietly answered, "Her name is Sarah Grace Beckwith, and I'm pretty sure she died in 1953. I think her dad was a businessman here. He got put in jail for bootlegging, a long time ago – I think it was in 1965. But it looks like she grew up and went to school here."

"How did she know your uncle?" Chad asked.

I took a deep breath. "I found a box full of letters in Fred's attic," I answered. "He hid it under the floorboards. The letters were from Sarah, along with a few pictures of her. I couldn't figure out where they met, but it looks like she was going to marry him after he got out of the Army."

Chad and Stephanie looked at each other in disbelief. "*She* was going to marry *him?*" Stephanie finally managed to ask.

"Yeah," I said. "That was in May of 1953. He moved here not too long after that, but he never got married, so I guess she died sometime later that year."

"Your uncle didn't come from here, did he?" Chad asked.

"No. My grandparents lived in Tuckerton. Fred moved to McDowell Mills right after he got back from Korea – literally the day after he got back. I don't know if she was still alive or not, but I guess she was, or he wouldn't have moved here." I thought about it. "I kind of hate to say it, but I think our best chance of finding out more is to ask her."

"You sure you want to do that?" Stephanie said. "I always thought she was interesting just because she seemed different from the others, but the way she acted towards you was kind of scary."

"I think I'll have to," I told her. "I'm pretty sure Fred either bought the farm from her dad, or bought it before he could. She told him her dad was looking to buy it. With that going on, and her dying around that time, it looks really suspicious. I'd rather ask her than someone else."

They both looked uneasy, so I changed the subject. "But before we ask her anything, I think we need to know more about what happened to her father, so we need to start looking for stories about his arrest, and see if we can find out what the other connections are."

"What do you think happened?" Chad asked.

"I don't know. But I know her dad, or someone else in her family, went to jail around 1965. You take this viewer and start looking in 1953, and see if you can find her obituary. I'm going to look for what happened to her dad."

"We can only request one roll of microfilm at a time," Stephanie objected. "And you have to have a library card."

I hadn't thought of that. "Guess I'd better apply for one now." I started to turn and go to the main desk, but she stopped me.

"The librarian likes us," she said, more quietly than before. "But the rule is, only one roll from the local paper at a time, so we'll find the obituary first. That'll be the easy part. If her dad was sentenced in 1965, he might have been arrested in 1964, so that'll take longer."

I couldn't argue with her logic, but I pointed out, "I'll still need to get a card."

She sighed. "OK, then," she said, and together we went to the checkout desk and looked around. No one was there, and there was no librarian in sight. There was a bell on the desk, and I was about to ring it when Stephanie hissed, *"don't!"*

I froze with my hand six inches above the bell. "Why?" I asked.

"Miss Roberts *hates* that bell," she replied.

"Oh," I said, slowly withdrawing my hand as the librarian – Miss Roberts, presumably – came out of one of the two offices behind the desk and looked at me with one raised eyebrow. She appeared to be about sixty, and looked almost exactly like what most people in that time thought a librarian should look like – thin, bookish, conservatively dressed, and an obvious spinster.

"Hello, Stephanie," she said in an aside, before returning her focus to me. "And who might this be?" she asked, looking at me as though I smelled bad.

"This is our friend Steve," Stephanie said. "He just moved here. He didn't know about the bell."

The librarian looked closely at me for a moment. My hand still hovered over the bell; realizing this, I belatedly drew it back. "You look like you could be Fred Smith's boy, but I can't imagine him having any children – whether he knew about them or not," she remarked.

"He was my uncle," I answered her. I wasn't especially friendly, but neither was she.

She nodded. "That would explain it," she said. Her attention shifted to Stephanie, and her inattention – if it could be called that – was very pointedly directed toward me. I could have threatened her with a baseball bat and I doubt she would have blinked. "What can I get for you?" she asked.

"We need the microfilm for the County Herald for 1953," Stephanie replied.

Miss Roberts nodded. "You find another one?" she asked.

"We're not sure yet," Stephanie answered. Miss Roberts turned without acknowledging me further and returned to her office. Stephanie glanced at me. "She knows a little about the ghosts, but she's never seen them," she said quietly. "She knows most of the history of the county, so she's been to all the places that are supposed to be haunted, but since she's never seen anything, she doesn't believe they're real. She thinks we go through the gravestones and try to find interesting or sad stories of people buried there, like Tommy."

"Oh," I replied. "Have you ever asked about Sarah before?"

"We didn't know who we were looking for, or when she died, so we never asked," she said, shrugging, as Miss Roberts re-emerged from her office with a circular cannister about three inches across and an inch thick. She looked at Stephanie as she handed over the cannister. "Does this new subject have a name?" she inquired.

Stephanie looked at me, and I replied, "Sarah Beckwith."

The librarian's face suddenly became wary, and if anything, even less friendly than before. "What do you know about her?" she asked, and her voice was almost a hiss.

"All we know is that she died in 1953, and one of her relatives was put in jail in the sixties for bootlegging," I answered. Miss Roberts studied me for a long time.

"Fred Smith died not too long ago," she said evenly, watching me as she spoke. "He moved here right before she died. Sarah loved that man, and she thought he loved her, until he came back from Korea. Something went wrong." Her eyes narrowed. "He ever tell you anything about it?"

"No, ma'am," I replied, looking straight back at her. "My uncle Fred and I hated each other. Fred pretty much hated everybody."

We matched stares for a few more seconds, and then her eyes softened very slightly. "Of course he did. But then, most people here hated him as well." Her posture didn't shift a millimeter, but she seemed to sag very slightly. "Sarah Beckwith was one of my best friends when I was in school. Nobody really knows exactly what happened to her, and I don't think you'll learn much from that microfilm, but you go ahead and look." She started to turn away.

"Miss Roberts?" I called after her. She halted, but didn't move.

"I'm sorry for what happened. My uncle had kept her letters and some old pictures of her, and I know she loved him. I think he loved her, too. She wouldn't have kept writing him unless he did." I paused. "And he wouldn't have kept all those letters and those pictures if he didn't love her."

Miss Roberts turned again to face me, a look of mixed wonder and horror on her face. "Not unless he felt guilty," she said softly. I couldn't think of anything else to say to that, and after a moment she returned to her office, closing the door behind her.

"I hope I didn't just cost us a chance to look up the bootlegging case," I said ruefully to Stephanie as we returned to the microfilm station. Chad was staring at us.

"I've *never* seen Miss Roberts look like that," he said wonderingly. "What just happened?"

"She was friends with Sarah in high school," Stephanie replied. His eyebrows raised.

"I didn't know she was ever even *in* high school," he said. "I thought she was born as a sixty-year-old librarian."

"Ssssh!" she hissed in reply, looking back toward the librarian's office, but the door remained closed. "She's already upset, and we still have to look up the bootlegging case!"

"Sorry," Chad said, and took the cannister from her. Opening it, he took out the roll of microfilm and began threading it into the viewer.

"We know she was still alive in May of 1953, and Fred moved down there when he got back from Korea just after that," I said. "Start with June of 1953, I guess."

The microfilm blurred across the viewer as Chad forwarded it through the first half of the year, slowing after a minute or so. The County Herald's headline read, "School Board Recognizes Honor Graduates." The date beneath the masthead read "Thursday, May 28, 1953."

We glanced through the story beneath the headline, until Stephanie gasped and pointed at one of the accompanying photographs, which was captioned, "MOST STUDIOUS – John Mayer and Eugenia Roberts." The girl in the picture wore the same mildly severe expression as our librarian. She even dressed the same way.

"No doubt who that is," Chad snickered, but my eyes had already drifted to the right, and I pointed toward another picture. Two photos to the right of Miss Roberts, Sarah smiled out at us beside a short, grinning, pleasant-looking male student. "FRIENDLIEST – Leonard Benton and Sarah Beckwith."

"Wow," Stephanie breathed. I couldn't speak. The girl in the picture had the same, brilliant smile as in Fred's photograph. No wonder she'd been named friendliest in her class – anyone would have liked that smile.

After a few seconds, Chad began scrolling again, though more slowly than before. After a few more issues – the paper was published three times a week – he fell into a rhythm of scrolling about twelve pages at a time, each time stopping at that day's obituary section. We had to scan each entry – there was no listing of names at the top – and so it took us nearly ten minutes to get through June.

Finally, in the first issue in July, we found what we were looking for:

"BECKWITH – Miss Sarah Grace, 18, of McDowell Mills passed away unexpectedly on Wednesday, July 1. A private ceremony will be held for the family at First New Jerusalem Methodist Church on Monday, July 6, with interment to follow in New Jerusalem cemetery."

That was all there was. We all looked at each other. Stephanie was biting her lip, and Chad looked puzzled and dismayed.

"I've never seen her gravestone," Stephanie whispered. "We need to go and find it."

"Yeah," Chad agreed, and began rolling up the microfilm. I looked out the window and groaned. It was noticeably darker outside than when we had arrived, and not because of the time. "We'd better hurry."

"Oh, no," Chad said, trying to rewind faster without damaging the strip. A minute later, it was back in its cannister and we were at the librarian's desk. The office door was closed. I looked at my friends, and then looked meaningfully at the bell.

"Don't," Stephanie whispered. I thought about it for a moment, and then took the cannister from her. Going around the desk, I approached the office door and knocked quietly.

Chad and Stephanie came up behind me. For almost a minute, there was no answer. We could hear the first grumblings of thunder outside.

Just as I was about to knock again, the door creaked open. Miss Roberts' expression had not changed, but there was a telltale redness in her eyes, and a very slight tremor in her jaw. She was still a bit scary, but more than anything else, I just felt sorry for her – almost as much as for Sarah.

I handed her the cannister and said, very quietly, "I'm sorry you lost your friend. I promise I'll try to figure out what happened to her."

Her jaw hardened for just a second, but then she sighed, and took the cannister from me. "I doubt you'll be able to, now," she said, her succinct voice dulled and flattened by sadness. "Too many bad things have happened here over the years. This is just one more. Her mother didn't last a year after she passed away. Her daddy died in prison, where he belonged, but that didn't change anything. The whole sheriff's office was run out for corruption, not too long after that, and a year later, the new department was worse than the old one." She gazed at me for a few seconds. "Your family must have taken over Fred Smith's old farm. Are you going to try to work it?"

"No, ma'am," I answered. "We're going to sell it, as soon as we can."

"Make sure you do," she said, shaking a trembling finger at me. "You and your family get out as fast as you can. It's not going to get better here. Not anytime soon. Now go on, and if you ever find out more, promise me you'll tell me about it before you go."

"I will," I whispered. She nodded at me, and then closed the door again. I turned around and walked past Chad and Stephanie, out from behind the desk and straight for the exit. The thunder rumbled again, nearer than before. We were all outside, and the wind was picking up, before any of us spoke.

"Where are we going?" Chad said loudly, trying to speak over the noise of the wind. A few big raindrops began to splash around us. Stephanie and I both gave him incredulous looks.

"OK, if you want to go to the cemetery, go right ahead, but I'm not getting out to find that grave. Not in this kind of storm. You guys can look if you want." He turned and started to climb into his truck.

"We can wait a little while for the rain to let up when we get there," I told Stephanie. "It'll blow over once the front of the line rolls through."

"I know," she answered. "And yeah, Chad's right. I'm not looking for the grave until this lets up some." As she ran around to the passenger side of his truck, I could see the line where the heavy rain was coming up the street, less than a hundred yards away. I bolted for my truck and slammed the door shut just as it arrived. Instantly, the windshield and windows became opaque, and praying that the truck's engine was sound, I started it up, leaving it in neutral until Chad and Stephanie had backed out and pulled onto Highway 255, heading north with me following them.

The rain continued to pound down as we drove, much more slowly than we ordinarily would. I hadn't thought to check the wipers on the truck, but fortunately, they worked. It took us almost twice as long as usual for us to get to New Jerusalem

Park, and even after we arrived, the rain was still coming down too hard for us to consider going out into it.

Maybe half an hour later, the storm finally slackened enough for us to get out and look around. Small pools of rainwater had formed in the depressions around the cemetery. I looked over at Stephanie and Chad.

"Didn't you guys say you mapped out this cemetery when you first found out about the ghosts?" I asked.

"We did," Stephanie replied. "But Sarah wasn't on our map."

"Do you think you might have missed it?" I pressed.

"Not on this side," Chad said. "We walked the entire plot, grave by grave. She's definitely not on this end, but if her dad was one of the town bigwigs, she might be on the other side. We've never done a full map on it."

"Didn't it occur to you that she might have come from that side?" I asked.

"Actually, it didn't." Stephanie was getting testy. "We've never seen her cross the road."

"The graves on this side are mostly new," I pointed out. "Mr. Abbott was one of the older ones, but if there was a scandal over his death…" my voice trailed away.

"They would have buried him away from everyone else," Chad finished. "And if Mr. Abbott was buried that far away in 1957, Sarah would probably be out here, too."

"Not only that," Stephanie added. "Remember? Sarah's dad was arrested for bootlegging all those years later. If he was into that, he was probably doing it all along, and everyone probably knew it. They probably wouldn't even let him bury her in any of the town churches."

I thought that was probably right, so I only answered, "Then either it's really close, on this side, or it's all the way across the highway."

"Yeah. You and Chad start checking each grave on this end. I'll go ahead to the other side."

We all climbed over the low fence and began picking our way around the puddles that had formed in and along the cemetery walkways. I tried not to step on any graves as I went, but I couldn't help walking across a few of them as I searched, and I always whispered, "Sorry" as I crossed them.

We went back and forth along the far end of the cemetery, finding nothing. I was on my third pass when I noticed a bit of iron latticework protruding above the line of shrubs that we assumed was the boundary of the graveyard, some thirty feet beyond the last grave, on the far side of the pathway that led around the plots' outside edges. Thinking it was a fence I hadn't noticed, I walked toward it.

On the far side of the path, the ground was much softer and wetter, and less carefully kept. A line of trees beyond the hedge shaded the area heavily. As I drew near to the fence, I could see that it actually formed a small enclosure, the size of a small family plot, with two plaques set in the ground.

A small gap in the overgrown shrubs, no more than a foot wide, indicated where the gate into the enclosure was set. I parted the overgrown branches as best I could, looking for the latch, which turned out to be rusted shut. I pried at it for a moment, but it was stuck.

Glancing around, I saw a rock about the size of a softball under the tree, moss- and mud-coated, but big enough for what I needed. A few seconds later, after first clawing my way back out of the hedge, then scooping the rock from the ground and shouldering my way back in, I began banging the rock against the latch as best I could.

It took about six or seven hard blows to snap the latch – it had rusted through and had grown brittle – and then I realized that I would have to pull the gate toward myself. As I struggled to get it open and squeeze around it, I caught a glimpse of the name – Beckwith – on one of the markers.

For a few moments, I stood frozen, staring at the name, before wedging the gate open with a great effort and sidling through, shouting, "Chad!" as I entered the long-neglected plot.

The larger memorial bore a broad plate with the family surname. Two smaller plates, side by side, memorialized Sarah's parents:

BECKWITH

WILLIAM RAYMOND
MAR 16, 1908
MAY 29, 1977

HELEN ROSE CROMLEY
NOV 19, 1909
JAN 6, 1954

For a moment, I felt a tug at my heart as I realized how young Sarah's mother had been when she died, before I remembered that Sarah herself had been younger still. I wondered whether Helen had died of a broken heart. From the look of the plot, Sarah had been her only child.

The day was growing darker again, and threatening more rain, and I heard Chad approaching the far side of the hedge, as I looked at last on Sarah's marker:

SARAH GRACE
JAN 4, 1935
JUL 1, 1953

"Oh my God, I never knew this was here," I heard Stephanie say breathlessly. I supposed Chad had signaled her, and for a moment I looked over the hedge to them where they stood, barely twelve feet away. Then their eyes grew wide, and fearful, and I knew she was there.

The rain was starting again. Sarah was watching me from where she stood, directly over her own gravestone, with the same faint expression of worry and despair as before. It hurt to see her face, knowing how much time had passed.

"Hello, Sarah," I said. Her eyes widened.

"I know you're not my Freddy," she said quietly. "But you look so much like him that at first I thought he had finally come for me."

"He's my uncle," I answered her. "Or he was. He died about two months ago. My father – his little brother – inherited his farm."

She watched me for a little while, as the rain began to intensify. "He wasn't buried here," she finally said. "Since you visited, I've been watching for him, but he's not here."

I didn't know what to tell her about that. Fred had been cremated, and was currently in an urn on our mantle until we could figure out what to do with him. It took a moment for me to realize the importance of what she had said.

"Sarah, what happened to you?" I asked her.

For just a moment, I saw a darkness in her eyes, and recoiled. She wasn't threatening me. It was just that some of the things she said were conveyed emotionally as much as verbally. Something awful and painful had happened.

"Bring Freddy to me," she said. And then she vanished.

At the same moment, another cloudburst hammered down on us. The trees around the plot sheltered us a little, but not much, and we were all too discombobulated by what had happened to care. I fought my way back through the hedge again, reclosing the gate as best I could, and together the three of us went back to our trucks through the rain.

CHAPTER FIVE

WE WERE BACK IN the old diner, dripping wet, waiting for another takeout order when Stephanie finally voiced the question in all of our minds: "How are we going to get Sarah together with your Uncle Fred?"

The silence that followed was our only answer. I couldn't figure out how I could get Fred's urn to the cemetery, and even if I found a way, I definitely couldn't leave it there. At least, not until I told my parents the whole story about Sarah, and even then, they'd probably have a lot of questions about what happened, and how I had found out. I couldn't tell them the entire truth. Not unless I wanted regular visits to a therapist, anyway.

"I haven't even seen a ghost of Fred," I remarked, glumly. "There may not be anything to reunite her with."

"And I don't know how we could bring them together, if you can't move the urn," Chad put in. I thought about that.

"D'you think she could ride in my truck?" I asked, with little enthusiasm. I wasn't exactly afraid of Sarah, but having her that close for the trip to the farm was extremely unsettling. From Stephanie's look at me, I could tell I wasn't alone.

"No one's seen them do anything really bad, except Pastor Samuels, and even that wasn't really him. It was the reaction he got," Chad finally said. "But we don't really know what they're capable of. I don't know if even *they* know. And if something happened, with you driving that truck…" he looked out the diner window. It was still raining pretty hard.

"Yeah. I don't think I want to do that. But we have to do *something*," I said. "If we don't, she might be here for another forty years. Or longer."

"Would you let her wait that long?" Stephanie asked me, with a look I hoped I didn't deserve.

"No," I answered. "But I might not be here very long. Once the farm is fixed up, Dad's probably going to sell it, and we'll move again. It might be a while before I can come back."

A different, but still unsettling, expression took over her face. Chad sighed. "But you're here for now, and really, she shouldn't have to wait any more. It'd be different if she was like Tommy, but she knows she's not alive. She's stuck here, permanently, unless we can figure out how they can move on."

Stephanie's eyes teared as he said this. I couldn't think of anything to add.

Our bags of food arrived as the rain slackened again. We took them outside, still not talking, and I got in my truck to go back home, when a thought came to me.

"I have an idea," I called to them as they got into Chad's truck to leave. They both looked over at me. Neither one said anything.

"Meet me at the park Monday morning, a little before seven," I called to them. "I'll bring the urn. If it works, we'll know pretty quick, and we can figure out what to do next."

"What if it doesn't work?" Stephanie asked.

"If it doesn't, then I can get the urn back to the house before it's missed, and we can try something else," I answered. They looked at each other, then back at me, and nodded as I got into the truck.

THAT SUNDAY DRAGGED dragged in a way that was even worse than usual. Like I said, we didn't attend church; even if Mom and Dad had been inclined to go, we didn't expect to be living there long enough to join one, and anyway, in McDowell Mills, your parents had to be buried there before you could be considered a full member in most of the churches.

I tried to while away the evening by watching the Braves game with my dad. I liked baseball well enough – and the Braves were finally a good team, after being terrible for almost my entire childhood. The national network had picked up the game for a Sunday night broadcast. Nevertheless, watching them play the Giants, who had just signed Barry Bonds and were loaded with great pitching, was just depressing. After the Giants knocked out the Braves' starter, taking a 6-0 lead in the third inning, I decided to go back through all the stuff I had found in the attic, and see if I'd missed anything.

I'd moved most of the receipts into one of my school folders so that no one would notice them. I knew why Fred had bought the flowers, of course, but I didn't know yet why he had stopped. I thought about that as I thumbed through the slips of paper, and then it came to me. Sarah's father had died in 1977, and had been buried in the family plot.

I looked again at the receipts, and snorted. They were from – I'm not kidding about this – Mammy Mammy's Floral Arrangements, and from the address, it looked like they had been located on the square in McDowell Mills. I couldn't remember seeing a florist in the square, but I also knew I'd probably never notice it even if it was there. It wasn't like I had any reason to buy flowers. Mother's Day was still several weeks away.

But now, I realized, I did have a reason. A *really* good reason.

The McDowell Mills phone book was barely larger than the spiral notebooks I used at school, split about evenly into White and Yellow Pages. It lay on the shelf in the kitchen where we kept our phone. As I thumbed through it, I hoped that Mammy Mammy was still in business, since all the other phone books had been thrown out when we cleaned out the house.

It turned out that there were three florists listed in the county, but only one in McDowell Mills, and it wasn't the one I needed. Mollie's Flowers and Gifts was in the same shopping center where I'd made a fool of myself learning how to drive my truck, and while I wasn't anxious to go back there, the advertisement in the book claimed that the shop had been open since 1961.

I only hoped that they would remember who their competition was back then. If the same woman, Mollie, was still running the shop, she might recall, but I knew I'd need to buy some flowers from her if I was going to ask her a lot of questions.

I looked again at the receipts. Fred had always bought a dozen white roses, every month. At least I knew what to get for Sarah's marker.

I picked up the phone and dialed. After a few moments of ringing, a low female voice answered.

"Hello, may I speak with Chad, please?" Yeah, I know. My mom would get so irritated with people who didn't use proper phone etiquette that she drilled it into my head from the time I was a little kid. She justified it by telling me she didn't want other kids' parents to think I was as rude as their own kids were. I secretly thought she was overreacting to her own pet peeve, but it was easier for me to go along than deal with her annoyance if she heard me doing otherwise.

"Yes, he's here. One moment." The response wasn't particularly friendly, but it wasn't rude, either. I hoped I hadn't interrupted anything important.

After a few seconds' worth of background noise, Chad picked up another phone, and I heard his mom hang up. "This is Chad," he said.

"Hey, it's Steve," I said. "After school tomorrow, can we go over to the florist's next to the grocery store on Macon Street? I've got an idea on how we might find out some more stuff."

"I thought we would find out when we bring her your uncle tomorrow," Chad said. He sounded a little nervous.

"If that works, then yeah," I hedged. "But what if it doesn't? I'm not sure it will, and if it doesn't, we'll have to try something else. But there's a bigger problem."

I heard him sigh over the phone. "You mean it gets worse? Great," he grumbled.

I glanced around quickly. Mom was still in the kitchen; Dad had gone to the bathroom while the TV was on a commercial break. I lowered my voice. "Why are there so many ghosts in that one place, and none anywhere else?" I asked. "You guys said yourselves that all the other supposedly haunted places in town were bogus. But New Jerusalem is real. There are *real* people – a *lot* of them – haunting that cemetery. There has to be a reason why."

"I dunno, Steve," Chad answered, lowering his voice in turn. "Until you showed up, the ghosts were just sort of there. We could find out stuff about them, you know, like who they were – even talk with some of them – but this thing with Sarah is different." The line went silent for a few seconds. Just as I was about to ask if he was still there, he spoke again. "Something *bad* happened to her. That whole family was messed up. Look where they were buried. There's graves on the church side of the highway that aren't that old. They got put out there for a reason."

"Her mom died young, too. But Sarah would have been the first one in the family to go, so they probably bought the plot when she died," I said.

"It's more than that. Stephanie told me that those are the oldest graves on that side of the highway," Chad replied. "So they were the first ones buried across the street, and they're still way back away from almost everyone else."

"Her dad was a bootlegger," I pointed out. "I don't think he was too welcome there."

"Yeah," Chad said. "So they put their plot way out across an empty field, and then after he died, they let the hedge grow up until no one could see them anymore."

That seemed kind of heartless to me, but then I remembered what some of the churches in McDowell Mills could be like. "That sounds right. And Fred stopped leaving flowers for her then, too." An ugly chill ran down my spine. "You think her dad's there? I mean, as a ghost? That might have stopped him from leaving the flowers."

"I dunno. But if that's true, it would mean your uncle knew about the ghosts, too." Chad paused. "Look, we aren't going to know until tomorrow. Maybe you should let this go until then."

He was right, but that was going to be easier said than done. "I know. I just can't get her out of my mind. She's been waiting for – for *something*, since my dad was a little kid. She could have been my aunt – she might even have been a grandmother by now." I was surprised at how much it hurt to think about it. "She has to know she missed – she missed *everything*."

"Yeah. And so did Tommy, and so did a bunch of the others," Chad pointed out. "How're we going to help Tommy find his ball? What do we do for Mr. Abbott? It looks like they stuck him out across the road, too." He fell silent, and I had no answers.

Or maybe I did.

"You said Mr. Abbott never talks to you. Have you ever talked to him? Or tried to find his family and find out what really happened?" I asked.

"Dude. You don't ask questions like that around here." Chad's voice was flat. "You have any idea how much bad stuff has been swept under the rug? When something goes down like what happened with the Sheriff's office, that only means that it got so out of hand that someone outside the county noticed it. That's probably why everyone thinks so many places here are haunted." He paused. "This has *got* to be the guiltiest place in America. People have been doing bad things here since – since there's been people here."

That definitely rang true. Even leaving out the redneck contingent that behaved as though the Civil War had never ended, and certainly not in defeat, there were too many little power networks in town that existed to benefit no one but themselves. My parents knew that as well as I did, and it was one reason why we didn't plan to stay there long.

"What if you and Stephanie say that you're doing a research paper on the town?" I asked. He snorted.

"We're juniors in high school," he answered. "No one's going to tell us anything, except maybe Miss Roberts, and it's not like she's real popular. How many people do you think actually use the library? Every couple of years, there's a fight on the county commission about whether to keep funding it. None of those people read. They don't even read their Bibles."

"Can't argue with that," I replied. I was trying to remember to keep my voice down, but I was starting to get mad. "But don't we have to try? It's bad enough that we deal with the lousy system here when we're alive. The people in that cemetery are *dead*, and they *still* have to deal with it. There's something really *wrong* with that."

"I know." Chad sounded defeated. "And now you get why so many kids leave here. This place *sucks*."

I sighed. "It does. But can you help me out tomorrow, in case the urn doesn't work?"

"I guess," he said. "But she wants you to bring your uncle to her. You haven't seen his ghost, have you?"

"Good grief, no," I replied. "I wouldn't stay in this house if I did."

"Then I don't know if any of this will work," Chad said. "But we'll give it a try. We bring the urn in the morning, and if that doesn't work, we ask about the flowers after school."

"OK. Thanks, Chad. See you tomorrow." I waited a beat, then hung the phone up and went back to my room. Studying wasn't going to take my mind off Sarah, but it would at least distract me until bedtime.

THE NEXT MORNING, I was roused by my alarm clock at ten minutes to six, and was in the shower in a matter of seconds. My best bet was to get ready before Dad got up, and borrow the urn early enough so that I could get it back after he left for work, but before Mom was dressed. If she heard me come back, I could say I forgot my wallet.

Less than twenty minutes later, I was showered, dressed, and in my truck. The urn was carefully packed behind my seat. I saw my parents' bedroom light come on as I turned the truck around in the driveway and drove out onto the road, and said a quick prayer to anyone who might be listening that Dad wouldn't notice Fred was missing.

It was still predawn by the time I reached New Jerusalem Park and pulled my truck up next to the fence. As I killed the engine, I saw a pair of lights turning in behind me, and hoped it was Chad and not a sheriff's deputy. By the time I had emerged from the cab, carrying Fred's urn, Chad and Stephanie had parked beside me and were getting out.

"I hope this works," Chad mumbled sleepily. Stephanie was yawning. I looked at them both and shrugged.

"Let's do this, then," I said, and climbed over the cemetery fence, being careful not to drop Fred. They followed. Less than two minutes later, we reached the hedge hiding the gate to the Beckwiths' plot. I looked back at my friends.

"Here goes nothing," I said, and pulling the gate open, I shouldered through the bushes. To my great surprise, Sarah was already visible, waiting for us. For the first time, I saw an expression other than desperation on her face, and it nearly broke my heart. She looked hopeful, almost unwillingly so. I made room for Chad and Stephanie to follow me in, then looked directly at her.

"I'm not sure this will work," I said quietly. The dawn was beginning to brighten in the east, behind us. Sarah still looked hopeful, but very sad.

"I don't know what I'll do if it doesn't," she answered. I tried to smile at her.

"There's something else we can try," I said. "If Fred doesn't show up now, there may be another way. Don't give up yet."

The look on her face then was so intense that it took my breath away. I realized that she must have been incapable of crying, because anyone living would have been in tears. I could feel thickness in my throat just from seeing her. A sniff from Stephanie told me that I wasn't the only one.

I placed the urn on her marker, carefully, and stood back. Silence fell as we all waited. The new day gradually brightened. Minutes ticked slowly by.

And nothing happened.

"He's not coming," Sarah said distantly. She looked like she was about to fade out.

"We'll come back this afternoon," I said quickly. "There's something else we have to look into after school today."

The desperate look had returned to her face. She nodded, and bowed her head. As respectfully as I could, I took the urn from her marker, and the three of us edged out of the plot again. It was nearly sunrise as we started back toward our trucks, but another voice stopped us.

"Mister, can you help me find my ball?"

Tommy was standing some twenty feet away from us, looking plaintive. Stephanie burst into tears, and as Chad put his arm around her, I glanced behind me. Sarah had followed us out of the gate, and was watching us. As I saw this, something else caught my eye, and turning back toward the church, I realized I couldn't breathe.

"Mister?" Tommy was walking toward me. Stephanie was crying openly. No one else, it seemed, had noticed what I was seeing.

I swallowed hard, and with my free hand, I pointed toward the church, somewhat above it. There, in the sky, what looked like a window into heaven itself had opened, streaming with white light that blended into the hues of the sunrise.

"Your ball's right there," I managed to say, pointing toward the window. Stephanie's crying ceased abruptly, and I heard Chad breathe, "Oh, my God."

Tommy turned half around, and saw the window. A broad smile broke across his features as he looked back at me. "Thanks, mister!" he cried, grinning, and began to run straight toward the window, rising above the ground higher and higher as he ran. In only a few seconds, he was lost against the brightness, and shortly after that, the window itself winked out, leaving only the reds and oranges of the sunrise behind it.

I looked back at Sarah again. She was still looking up into the sky, at the place where the window had been.

"You're waiting for Fred, so that you can go together," I said aloud. She turned toward me, staring full into my eyes for a moment, and nodded, fading out as she did.

Stephanie gulped, trying not to start crying again. Chad and I glanced at each other.

"We have to help her," he said. "We have to help all of them."

"At least we know what that help looks like, now," I said. Then I remembered the urn I still held.

"Oh… *crud*!" I shouted, and broke into a run toward the parking lot, calling "I'll see you at school!" over my shoulder as I vaulted over the fence. A minute later, I was on the road again, trying not to speed as I headed back home.

The drive definitely took several minutes less than it should have. Fortunately, no police cars spotted me. I pulled into the driveway and killed the engine, muttering a silent thanks that my dad had already left. Grabbing the urn from where I had tucked it away, I sprinted into the house, replacing it on the mantle only a few seconds before my mom came in from the kitchen.

"Steve! Why are you back here?" she asked, a little more forcefully than I was comfortable with. I ran toward my room, calling back over my shoulder, "I forgot my wallet."

Less than a minute later, I was heading back out the door toward my truck, when my mom called to me from the porch. I stopped, halfway between the front stoop and the driveway, and slowly turned around. I was breathing like I'd run a race, and felt like it, too.

"Steve, are you all right? You seem like you've been a little off over the past week," Mom said. I closed my eyes and took a deep breath, letting it out slowly.

"I'm fine, mom. Only I'm going to be late. We went in early to work on a Chemistry lab, and I realized I didn't have my wallet, so I came back for it." I tried to slow my breathing while she studied me.

"You know we aren't going to stay here. As soon as we can sell this place, we'll be gone. You *do* understand that, don't you?" she asked.

"I know, Mom," I replied, trying not to look as stressed as I felt.

She looked at me for what felt like a long time, as if she wanted to say something else but couldn't quite figure out how to say it. The only thing she actually said was, "All right, you be careful. I'd rather you were late than get a ticket for speeding."

"Yes, Mom," I answered, and I meant it. I got back in my truck, gunned the engine, and headed off to school again.

CHAPTER SIX

"YOU THINK THIS florist is going to know anything about your uncle?" Stephanie asked me that afternoon, sitting between me and Chad as we rode together in Chad's truck to the same strip mall where I had learned to drive mine.

"No idea," I answered. "But this place has been open long enough that the owner might be able to help, and anyway, I want to put some flowers on Sarah's grave. No one's paid any attention to their plot in years."

"Just be careful," Chad admonished me, as he turned the truck into the parking lot and looked for a spot near the florist's. "This town has a lot of bad history. For all we know, Mollie or whoever might have hated Mammy Mammy's guts."

That sounded very true to form for McDowell Mills. I would have been even more worried, but I had learned that a lot of the businesses in town were still run by the old families that had started them, fifty or even a hundred years ago. If the story of Sarah's death had become a local legend, the older generation might remember it even if – like Miss Roberts – they weren't anxious to tell us much.

Chad parked the truck almost directly in front of the florist's shop. We all climbed out and made for the entrance, but Stephanie stopped us right in front of the glass doors, glaring at each of us in turn.

"Let me do the talking," she said. Chad and I looked at each other and shrugged.

"Fine with me," I answered. "I look too much like Fred anyway. I'd probably just make this harder."

Stephanie nodded emphatically at me before turning and entering the shop. Chad and I followed.

I don't know what I expected to see inside, but whatever that was, I was radically incorrect. The usual florist's shop in a small town – at least back then – was always decorated in a cheap, unfashionable country-style motif. Mollie's wasn't that at all. The floor and walls looked like Mondrian paintings with an art-deco accent, but with a Seventies look as well. The design looked somehow dated, even though the whites were bright and unfaded, the colors – primarily blue, red and yellow – were sharp, and there wasn't a speck of dust anywhere. The most amazing thing was, even with all the flowers and plants on display, and despite the starkness of the décor, it all worked. It looked strange and beautiful and yet old.

"Cool!" Stephanie breathed. She obviously had the same take on the place as I did.

"This is *weird,*" Chad said softly. We glanced at each other again before making our way toward the back of the store. Behind the sales counter stood a thin, suited black man, about thirty-five years old, as dustless and impeccable as the shop itself. He was poring over a catalog as we approached, but glanced up when we reached the counter. I noticed his name tag, which read, "Ambrose."

"How can I help you?" he asked. He had a very deep, but very soft voice. I'd have bet he could sing a baby to sleep in under a minute.

Stephanie smiled toward him. "Are you the shop owner?" she asked.

He looked at her with one eyebrow arched, and then tapped his nametag. "Do I look like a Mollie to you?" he asked, sardonically but not unkindly.

"Of course not," she replied. "But with some of the older shops in town, they keep the name after the original owner retires, and this store's been here thirty years, so I wasn't sure if Mollie was still the owner."

"So you don't know Mollie," the man replied patiently, "but you want to speak to the shop owner. I've never seen you in here before. Do you mind if I ask what this is about?"

"It has to do with something that happened a long time ago. Before this store even opened. We've been researching some of the people buried at New Jerusalem cemetery, and we found an old plot with a really strange story that we're trying to figure out," Stephanie answered.

Ambrose's eyebrow lifted again. "There's no shortage of dead people with strange stories in this town," he intoned, as softly as before. "And as we're florists, we tend to be involved in those stories right after the part where those people get dead." He leaned across the counter, closer to us, and continued, "Some of those stories are probably best forgotten." His eyes settled on me for a moment, and I saw just a flicker of uncertainty in them.

I spoke quickly, before Stephanie could open her mouth to reply. "You're probably right about most of them. But I've learned something about a girl that's in that plot. She and my uncle were in love with each other and wrote to each other while he was in Korea. They were going to marry, but she died right after he got back."

Ambrose looked at me for a long time. I could tell that he was studying me, but he looked faintly puzzled as well. I wasn't sure what to make of that. Finally, he stood up straight again, leaning back slightly as he crossed his arms and frowned.

"My mother opened this shop," he said in his soft voice. "She works in the back now, doing the books. She might be able to tell you more." He looked around at all three of us. "But I think she'd appreciate it if you were to – make a purchase here, if you understand me." He gave me a significant look.

I looked around the shop. I had about forty dollars in my wallet, and from what I could see, the flowers I wanted would cost most of what I had.

I realized I didn't care. Sarah needed this. I was just beginning to understand why Fred had been so awful; if she had been my girlfriend, and then died, I would have hated the world, too.

"I'll take a dozen white roses," I said. Ambrose nodded, and without saying more, he turned and walked through a curtain behind the sales counter.

"Do you have enough money for that?" Chad asked me.

"Barely," I answered. "If you could kick in a few bucks, that would help."

I could hear Ambrose speaking with a woman in the back, but their voices were both too soft to hear clearly. Chad dug in his pocket for his wallet and drew a ten-dollar bill from it, handing it to me just as Ambrose re-emerged through the curtain. He was accompanied by a woman who resembled him about as much as I looked like Uncle Fred. Mollie looked as though she was dressed for church, and the severity of her expression as she looked at me – she barely noticed Chad and Stephanie – was also very church-appropriate. Her nose lifted slightly as she glared, as though I smelled bad.

"I know Fred Smith didn't make any copies of himself, but you're his spitting image," she said, in a soft voice midway between a drawl and a growl.

"He was my uncle," I replied. "He and I hated each other."

"Well, then, maybe you're not all bad," she replied, through her expression was still suspicious. "Who are you buying white roses for?"

I don't know how I knew it, but somehow, it was obvious to me that *she* knew who they were for. I hoped she could tell me more about why.

"Sarah Beckwith," I answered her.

She nodded. "That was who your uncle bought them for, though Lord knows he never bought them from me. He never did me anything but harm. I opened this shop after he drove my husband out of business."

"I don't know anything about that," I said. "But I can definitely believe he did that, if you say so. That was the sort of thing I'd have expected of him."

Her eyes narrowed. "You don't know about that story?" she asked.

"The only thing I know is that he was in love with Sarah Beckwith, and she with him," I answered her. "After she died, he left her a dozen white roses on her gravestone, every month.

That went on until her father died. I don't think anyone had visited their graves since then, until we found them yesterday."

Mollie's eyes had widened, and she had recoiled from me very slightly. "They were in love with each other? How on earth would you know a thing like that?" she asked.

"I have the letters she wrote to him, while he was in Korea," I answered. "They were planning to get married after he got out of the army. He bought his farm intending for them to live there, but she died before any of that could happen."

"You have the letters?" she asked, softly even for her.

"Yes," I answered.

"And you're *sure* that that's what was going on?" she asked.

I wanted to look over at my friends, but something told me to stay focused entirely on her. "Absolutely. She was already planning their wedding for when he came home."

Mollie's severe expression had dissolved into puzzlement and dismay. She was looking away from me, out the window at the front of the store, shaking her head slightly.

"This doesn't make any sense," she finally said, before regaining her focus on me. "How much do you know about how Sarah died?" she asked.

"I know it was on the first of July in 1953," I answered. "I don't know much else. I don't know if it was an accident, or if she got sick suddenly."

Mollie's eyes were boring into me again, but there was a haunted look to them. "She was shot to death in her own home," she told me. "My husband was a gardener and landscaper, and he was working that day at the Beckwith house. He saw Fred Smith show up just before noon, dressed real nice and looking like the happiest man in the world. He didn't stay happy long." She paused. "Not fifteen minutes later, he heard an argument inside the house. The windows were open. It sounded like Beckwith and Fred Smith were having a big disagreement, but he couldn't make out what they said.

"Then he heard the girl's voice join in, and it sounded like she was trying to get the other two to calm down, but her daddy kept shouting, and that's when he heard the shot." She waited for me to respond to that, but I was numb. No wonder Sarah was a ghost. Her own father had shot her. There was no chance Fred would have done it.

"The sheriff came, and took a statement from Ambrose – not my son here, but his father – and from Fred Smith, and from Mr. Beckwith. Everything got hushed up after that. All it said in the Herald was that she 'died suddenly.' I guess being shot by her racketeering father wouldn't have read too well, even if it was an accident." She was looking hard at me now. I was still too horrified to speak, but now I understood what happened. I knew why Fred had kept track of what Beckwith did.

"I'm almost positive Fred was the one who tipped off the GBI about Beckwith," I answered her.

She looked appraisingly back at me. "Then why did he tell my husband to quit his business and leave town?" she asked.

"I think he was working with Beckwith, trying to get dirt on him," I answered her. "I had thought he started working with him after Sarah died because they were almost family, and maybe old man Beckwith had sort of adopted him. But I don't know, now." I was thinking aloud. "Unless he realized that the sheriff was in Beckwith's pocket and decided to play along with the cover-up, and live to fight another day."

"That doesn't answer my question," she said suspiciously.

"Your husband was the only other witness," I said. "He could have caused a lot of problems for Beckwith if he started talking. If Fred was trying to bring him down from the inside, your husband might have made that impossible if he started broadcasting what happened to Sarah."

"Maybe so," she said. "He always said that Fred Smith made it seem that Beckwith was the one who wanted him gone." She sighed. "As it turned out, it didn't matter. Ambrose had a heart attack in 1959, and after that, he couldn't work anymore. He stayed around awhile longer, long enough to see his son graduate high school, and then died in his sleep two nights later."

"Fred left him alone after the heart attack?" I asked. She looked hard at me for a second before nodding affirmatively.

"Ambrose was – was not the same man after that," she said slowly. "I supposed that they didn't see him as a threat."

I didn't know how to answer that. I looked over at Stephanie.

"Thank you, Miss Mollie," she said, receiving a slight frown in response.

"Now you know the story behind those graves. It might be best if you just leave them alone now. This town's got plenty of ghosts without you stirring up more," she replied.

I tried to smile at her, but it wouldn't come, so I just nodded. Mollie looked back at me.

"For years I despised Fred Smith for what he did to my family," she whispered. "But I suppose now it was inevitable.

If Fred hadn't told Ambrose to leave, someone else working for Beckwith would have. That other someone might not have shown the same restraint. And now I understand why he was the man he was. By the time Beckwith was made to pay for his crimes, Fred Smith was the only man in the county that might have been hated as much as he was. He was a bitterly hard man." As she spoke, she approached me slowly, and reached out to me with a thin, veined hand that she placed on my shoulder.

"For years I was afraid to go home to the Lord. Afraid, because I could never forgive Fred Smith for what he'd done." Her voice didn't waver, but she swallowed just slightly. "Because of you three, I can understand, and I can forgive him now, and I can go home to glory." She patted me on the shoulder twice as the ghost of a smile passed across her face, and then turned around, making her slow way back to her desk.

"Thank you," I said, as we turned to leave. I felt as though I had just run a race. As we passed through the curtain, her soft voice floated back to us: "Don't forget to pay for those roses."

I glanced over to Chad. He was grinning, and somehow, we felt all of the tension that had been building in us release. Stephanie sighed, and I replied, half over my shoulder, "we won't, ma'am."

RIDING BACK TO the school to collect my truck, we were quiet for a while, mulling over what we had learned. I was still trying to grasp the idea that my uncle wasn't quite the horrible man I had always thought he was.

"I would never have guessed I'd ever feel sorry for Fred Smith," Stephanie finally said, breaking our silence. Evidently I wasn't the only one.

"But what can we do now?" Chad asked. "We know most of the story about them now, and it's no wonder she's a ghost, but until she's reunited with Fred, she's stuck here."

"And Fred's nowhere to be found," I put in glumly.

No one spoke for the rest of the drive. I hopped out in the school's parking lot. Stephanie rolled down her window as she slid over from the middle to the passenger seat.

"We'll take the roses to Sarah on the way home. Call us if you think of anything," she said. Her expression looked much like Sarah's had – sad and faintly desperate. I only shrugged and nodded in reply, because I had to swallow a lump in my own throat.

As I drove home, I kept trying to think of some way to help Sarah, but I was out of ideas. All I could see was her face, imploring me to find some way to reunite her with Fred, but I just couldn't see any way to do it if Fred wasn't a ghost, and if he was, he hadn't seen fit to turn up.

Mom had already made supper when I got home. I didn't really notice what I was eating, or talk much while we ate, and Mom watched me worriedly. As I stood to leave, she stopped me.

"Steven, what's going on? You've barely spoken to us this week." As she said this, Dad looked up at me, looking slightly puzzled, but attentive.

"Chemistry lab, Mom. I was ahead of the class on most of what they're doing, but we didn't do thermodynamics before I transferred, and I'm having to learn it now. I don't want Chad and Stephanie to get a bad grade because of me." I hated lying to Mom, and I think she knew I wasn't telling her anything like the whole story.

She continued to watch me for a few seconds, not saying anything, waiting for me to react to her scrutiny. I kept my face as still as I could. I really don't like lying.

"Is there anything else to this?" she finally asked me. "Are you in some kind of trouble?"

I sighed with relief. Whatever she thought was going on was far from the reality, and I wanted to keep it that way.

"No trouble," I answered truthfully. "Just worried about keeping my grades up. It'd look really bad if I trashed my grade-point average going to school here."

"He's right about that," Dad interjected. "Is it just Chemistry, or are you having trouble in your other classes?"

"Just Chemistry, and it's just this one section," I said. "The next two chapters are all stuff I already did."

Dad frowned, and glanced at Mom. "You're not having any problems with living here? You know we're moving again as soon as we can sell this place."

"I know. Mom said the same thing this morning. But I don't like anything that had to do with Uncle Fred," I replied. There was at least some truth to that. "I know he never liked me."

"He didn't like anyone," Mom said, looking at Dad.

Dad nodded. "Well, regardless of that – have you finished your homework? It sounds like you need to do some studying."

"I'm going to. Right now, if that's okay."

Mom sighed. I usually helped her clear up after meals, and I felt guilty that I wasn't offering to help her this time. "It's all right. I'll get the dishes for tonight. You go make sure you get caught up on your classwork."

I nodded in agreement, then stood up and left the kitchen. I could feel them watching me leave, but no one said anything.

I went back to my bedroom and flopped on the bed, closing my eyes for a moment, trying to let the tension and worry about Sarah drain out of me, but I kept coming back to the same conundrum.

There were so many ghosts at the church, including Sarah, but not Fred – even when I brought his urn there. Why was that?

I understood why Tommy would have been there; he had died on the same road that split the cemetery. But the others had all died in different places, including Sarah. Even the ones that didn't follow the crowd into the church each evening were still in that graveyard.

It didn't make sense, I suddenly realized. The ghosts shouldn't have been in the churchyard; they should have been in the places where they had lived, or where they had died. Why would they haunt the place where they were buried?

And could they leave it, if they chose to? Could they even make that choice?

I felt like I was thinking in circles, but one thing had become clear to me – we needed one more piece of information from Sarah. We needed to know how she had reached the New Jerusalem churchyard in the first place.

I thought for another minute, and then went back into the living room to call Chad. My Dad gave me an odd look as I went to the phone.

"I'm going to meet Chad and Stephanie tomorrow for breakfast, and go over this again." Dad nodded, and I picked up the receiver, dialing Chad's number. Mercifully, he picked up the phone on the second ring. "Hello?"

"Chad, it's Steve. I think we should meet again tomorrow morning for breakfast, and then go over this stuff again. It's still not making sense, but I'm beginning to understand some of it, and I wanted you two to sort of guide me through it."

Chad knew what I was really talking about, and his voice lowered. "You got another idea for helping Sarah? Good. Stephanie's really upset about her."

"Yeah, me too," I answered, trying not to betray my emotions. "But I think I'm almost there. There's a couple of basic principles I don't think I understand. If we can't solve them, we may have to ask Miss Beckwith." I held my breath, hoping my Dad wasn't paying too much attention.

"Gotcha. You want to meet at the park?"

"We'll meet at Cleve's," I said. "We'll need time to eat, and we can get into the school at seven. We'll meet about six-fifteen. Can you call Sarah and let her know?"

"Sure," Chad replied. I hoped he knew what I meant – that he should go back to New Jerusalem and let her know we would be coming the next morning.

"Okay, see you then. Bye." I hung up the phone, and looked over at Dad, who was lying back in his recliner. "I'm going early tomorrow to meet my friends, and then we'll head over to the school."

"All right, son," he replied. "I'm not feeling too good right now. Didn't feel great when I came home, and it's getting worse. I might be staying home tomorrow."

"Well, I hope you feel better," I replied. Dad's being home wouldn't make any difference, but I did want him not to be sick. I went back to my bedroom, pulled out my Chemistry text, and began rereading the section I had pretended not to understand. I was trying not to become obsessive about Sarah. More to the point, I knew reading the textbook would have me ready to sleep quickly enough that getting up early wouldn't be a problem.

CHAPTER SEVEN

THE FOLLOWING MORNING, I backed my truck out of the gravel driveway at exactly six o'clock, and drove into McDowell Mills on roads that were nearly empty. I was glad for that, because the sky was overcast and promised rain. Chad and Stephanie were already waiting for me by the time I pulled into Cleve's. Thankfully, they were already open. There were plenty of people in town who were up before sunrise, mostly heading to work, and the diner did pretty brisk business with the early morning crowd.

"We saw Sarah last night when we brought the roses. She knows we're coming. So what's your idea?" Chad asked as soon as I got out of the truck.

"How come there are so many ghosts in that cemetery?" I asked in return. "All the other haunted places in town – supposedly haunted, anyway – are in places where people died. No one died at New Jerusalem. Well, Tommy did, but he's gone now. But the others - how did they get there?"

Chad and Stephanie looked at each other. "We thought that it was because of their theology. It's in First Thessalonians, I think," Chad answered. "Something about how in the end times, the dead in Christ will rise first."

I looked at him incredulously. "Do you really believe that?"

"No!" Stephanie interjected, forcefully. "But maybe *they* believe it, so that's where their ghosts manifested. At least, that's what we thought."

"And if your uncle didn't believe it, he wouldn't manifest there," Chad added. "He might not have become a ghost at all."

"That's what I'm afraid of," I said. "But I had one more idea. We couldn't bring Fred to Sarah, but maybe we can bring Sarah to Fred."

They looked at each other. "How? We don't know where Fred is, and even if we did, I don't think Sarah can ride in a truck," Chad said.

"I know." I looked first to Chad, then Stephanie. "I'm going to have to walk with her back to the farm. If Fred's not there, I don't know what will happen. I can't think of anything else that would work."

"You're going to miss school?" Stephanie asked. "You know the sheriff's office will stop you if they see you out during school hours."

"I know," I said glumly. "But it's the only way it can work. If I try it at sunset, we'll be walking for hours at night. It's safer in the daytime. Besides, if I walk back to the house from New Jerusalem in the dark, my folks will freak out, and they'll want to know why I didn't call someone."

"How will you know if she's following you?" Chad asked. "We usually don't see them in the daytime."

"Look, we're wasting time," I said. I was getting impatient. "We need to get out to the cemetery. I need to be walking back with her before school starts."

"How long will it take for you to get back to your place?" Stephanie asked.

I thought about that. "I can take Airstrip Road back, so I won't have to go near town," I said. "It's about six or seven miles total from there. But I don't know if Sarah can follow me, and if she can, I don't know how fast she can go."

"At least there's more shade along the road going that way," Chad said. "Even in the day, we can see the ghosts if there's shade, or if it's –"

"Cloudy," I finished for him. "I don't know if the sunlight fades them out or not. It might be like AM radio, where the sun drowns out a lot of signals."

"I never thought of that," Stephanie said, surprised. "You can hear radio stations all over the southeast out here at night, but only the Atlanta stations in the daytime – them and the local station."

"And no one under sixty listens to the station in town," Chad put in. "That's weird, though. Maybe that's why most ghost sightings are at night – the sun drowns out their energy during the day."

I nodded. "But I've got to eat something if I'm going to hike seven miles, especially in the rain. Let's get some biscuits or something and go. Now."

Five minutes later, we left the diner with our breakfasts. A few drops of rain were falling, but fortunately, it was much lighter than the cloudburst that had accompanied our previous visit. I drove carefully through the slightly heavier traffic in town, stuffing as much food into my mouth as I could chew each time I had my shifting hand free. I didn't know whether Sarah would take offense to me eating, given her condition, but I didn't want to risk it.

We made our way north out of McDowell Mills to New Jerusalem, and pulled into the park a few minutes after six-thirty. We didn't stop to talk this time; as soon as we got out of our trucks, we went straight over the fence, and made a beeline to the hidden plot where the Beckwith family lay.

The hedge was damp from the light rain, soaking my shirt, but I didn't hesitate, pulling open the iron grating and forcing my way in. The roses had been placed in the vase built into Sarah's marker. As Chad and Stephanie followed me, Sarah reappeared. Her face bore a resigned look.

I got right to the point. "Sarah, we think there might be another way to bring you and Fred together, but we need to know a few things first. What do you remember since you died?"

I knew I was being too blunt, but I needed to know, as quickly as possible. I was thankful to see that she didn't seem to be offended by my question.

"I remember it was like waking up, from sleepwalking. All of a sudden, I was standing in our old house, in the parlor, and the ambulance was there." Sarah's bright outline became slightly fuzzy as she thought. "I realized what had happened. Freddy had already left the house. I didn't want to stay there anymore after what my daddy had done.

"I walked to Freddy's farm, the one he'd just bought, and stayed there a little while. He could see me, but it upset him, so after that, I just wandered around town until I learned about the ghosts here," Sarah continued. "There were kids here, even years ago, who would come to see the ghosts – just like you.

"Freddy came to visit me once every month. I remembered how sad seeing me had made him, so I stayed away when he came. I wanted him to be happy, and have a good life, but he never married, and every year, he seemed more bitter and sad. Finally, when my father died and was buried here, Freddy stopped coming. I had to let him be." She looked so sad that I had to swallow hard to keep from choking up. Stephanie sniffled behind me.

"I waited for him to come back again, or for him to die, so that we could leave the world together. When you came –" she pointed a finger toward me – "I wanted to believe you were him, and that it was time for us to go. I knew you weren't really Freddy, because you're alive, but I wanted it to be true anyway." Sarah had dimmed slightly. Behind the rain clouds, the sun was beginning to rise.

We were wasting time, and I needed to cut to the chase. "Sarah, can you ride in a truck?" I asked.

"No," she replied. "The only way I can travel is by walking."

"Can you travel in daylight?" I pressed her. Sarah frowned.

"I can, but you may not be able to see me," she answered.

I glanced up at the sky again. "If we leave now, I'll be able to see you. These clouds probably won't break before noon."

"What if it rains?" Stephanie objected.

"Shoot. I don't have an umbrella in the truck." I looked at Chad. "Do you have one I could borrow?"

"No," he replied. "And we're running late. I wouldn't be able to get back here with one without cutting first period." He frowned with chagrin. "I know I'm wimping out on you, but – couldn't you wait until this afternoon?"

I looked at Sarah again. Her face made my heart ache. I finally understood why my uncle had become the man he had been, but there was one thing I still didn't understand.

"Sarah, you saw what happened with Tommy. All the people here –" I waved indefinitely toward the cemetery – "all of them, they could go home like he did. Why do they all stay here?"

She smiled, but that only made her sadness more evident. "Some of them don't want to revisit the pain at the end of their lives. I wouldn't want to, for myself. It's not much of a – much of an afterlife, I guess, but it's familiar to them, and it's safe, and it's always the same." She looked out past us; I realized she could probably see through the hedge. "This town was built on a foundation of guilt and crimes. For most of the people here, who spent their lives here, it's too sad to remember. This isn't heaven, but it's close enough for most of them."

I took a deep breath. Sarah had affirmed much of what I believed – what *we* believed – about McDowell Mills. "Are you willing to take one more chance?" I asked her.

She looked soberly at me for a long time. An odd breeze had puffed up, warmer than it should have been for that time of morning and that time of year. I knew it was going to rain again, but I just didn't care. I wanted to do this.

"What will I do if we get there, and there's nothing waiting for me?" she asked.

She had waited so long, and endured so much, that I couldn't immediately answer her. I covered my face for a moment, willing myself not to start crying, and breathed deeply several times. Finally, I answered her, thickly: "I will promise you this much – until you find your way to the same home

Tommy's gone to, I will *never* stop trying to help you get there. *Ever.*"

"And if I'm – I'm not meant to go there?" Sarah's voice cracked as much as mine had. I realized for the first time how afraid she was. I glanced toward Chad and Stephanie; as grieved as they were for her, they were still surprised by her response.

I would have held her hands right then, but of course, I couldn't. I held mine out anyway. I knew her touch might be unpleasant, and I didn't care – but I was still surprised when she came closer and held her hands over mine, lightly contacting them. I could feel a coolness, and a slight, electric jolt, but it wasn't bad at all, and I managed not to flinch. We stared directly at each other. For the first time in my life, I genuinely envied my uncle.

"Sarah, any heaven that wouldn't have you is a heaven not worth going to. We *will* help you find your way home, no matter what. Won't we?" I looked back at my friends again; they both nodded.

I looked back at her. She was biting her lip, but her eyes were grateful, and there was just the tiniest spark of hope in them. She was going to try again – I knew it.

I looked back once more. "Guys, I got this from here. You go on ahead to school. I'll let you know what happens."

Stephanie's eyes teared again. "Okay." Her eyes shifted to look past me. "Sarah, I'm so glad to have known you." Her voice was cracking, too. "I just hope, for your sake, that this is goodbye."

"Me too, Sarah," Chad chimed in. "But if it isn't, it's like Steve said. We won't ever give up."

Sarah didn't answer them, but she managed a small, grateful smile, and gave them a small wave of her hand. "All right. Thanks, guys. See you when it's done," I said, nodding to them both, and as they turned to leave, my eyes met Sarah's again. "You know where the farm is. We can walk together, at least as long as it's raining."

"Rain doesn't bother me," she answered. "But is it a good idea for you to be out in this weather? It could make you sick."

"I know," I replied. "I'm sorry, and it might be wrong for me to say so, but I understand a lot more about my uncle now. I don't want you to wait even another day. It's time. You deserve this. Both of you do." It felt strange to identify with Uncle Fred, but all I had to do was look at Sarah, and it made sense.

She smiled at me again, but this time, it was the smile she might have given me if she had been the Aunt Sarah I never had. It was all right, though. She was someone you couldn't help but love, but also as unreachable as the gods on Olympus. Still, she needed me to make this last, short journey with her.

I took another deep breath. "So. Shall we go?"

She smiled again, and nodded, and we left her plot together, making for the highway.

WE WENT SLIGHTLY NORTH, out of our way, before turning along an old, abandoned road leading east into the woods behind New Jerusalem Church. The grounds were empty; the ghosts slept, and the living had yet to arrive. Neither of us spared the church more than a glance.

The pavement we followed was cracked and overgrown, little more than a single-lane path. In a few more years, the woods would reclaim it altogether. But it served my purpose, cutting off the long detour to the north that I would otherwise have had to take to reach Airstrip Road. It also kept me out of sight from passing deputies.

The clouds scudded overhead, not quite heavy enough with rain to dampen our walk, but dark enough to keep Sarah visible. It turned out that we could walk at about the same speed, luckily; I had worried that I might lose her if the day brightened too much. As it turned out, both she and the weather ensured that wouldn't happen.

We didn't speak as we walked. I couldn't think of anything to say that wouldn't sound trite or childish, but I did glance over at her from time to time, just to make sure she was keeping pace. Occasionally our eyes would meet, and she would smile at me. Always.

One hour later, we reached Airstrip Road. We were more than halfway back to the farm, and the rain finally started. I checked the sky again, and this time, the cloud cover meant business. I looked over at Sarah.

"I hope you weren't kidding about not being bothered by rain," I said. "It's probably going to be pretty heavy."

"It doesn't affect me," she answered. "But if you need to go faster, I can still keep up with you."

I nodded and tried to increase my pace. The rain seemed to take that as a challenge, and increased its intensity accordingly. I halted for a moment, looked up again, and then shrugged. If I caught a cold, I caught a cold – there wasn't anything I could do about that.

We trudged on as fast as I could manage, turning off Airstrip Road onto North Sardis Church Road, and following it for another fifteen minutes until we reached Sardis Baptist Church. We were less than three miles from the farm, but we had to cross one more state highway. It ran beside the church, and traffic on it was heavy. I groaned silently to myself, looking east at the line of headlights approaching the intersection where the two roads crossed. It needed a traffic light, but as was typical of all things McDowell Mills, the city fathers had yet to approve one. Usually, a traffic fatality was required for them to change anything road-related. I sincerely hoped I wasn't going to give my life just to put a light there.

"Have to wait to cross here," I said, as we neared the crosswalk. "I may have to run across, because the traffic's so heavy. If that happens, I'll wait till you're back with me before I keep going."

Sarah didn't answer, and after a few seconds I looked over at her; she was staring resolutely ahead. I realized she was beginning to dread what she would find – or wouldn't find – when we arrived. I tried to smile, but I think my face was beginning to look as desperate as hers did.

"No matter what happens, I won't give up. I promise." We had reached the crossing. A gap in the cars approaching from the left would reach us in a few seconds. I looked to the right, and I saw that we could cross then, if I hurried. I glanced at Sarah again. She nodded to me.

The last car on the left went by. I moved across the first lane, trying to time my arrival at the centerline with a gap on the right. It worked, but it was close; the next car on my left wasn't about to slow down, and whooshed less than three feet behind me as I ran to cross the remaining lane.

I looked back at the offending vehicle, willing myself not to give it the single-finger salute, and then saw Sarah beside me again.

"Let's go," I said, and continued south. We had almost another wet hour of walking in front of us.

TWO MILES AND TWO turns later, we were finally on the country lane leading to Fred's farm. The way was overhung with trees, which might have sheltered me from a lighter rainstorm, but this one was heavy enough that the trees seemed to act as gathering points. Fewer, but much heavier, drops splashed on and around me as we walked down the last hill. The road paralleled Fred's old cow pasture, now empty and overgrown beyond the trees that lined the way. I could see our driveway ahead.

I looked over at Sarah one last time. Her fear was plain to see in her expression, and though she had kept up with me, I had the sense that she was somehow lagging, reluctant to come any closer.

"It's time," I whispered. I didn't know if she could hear me over the rain, but she stayed beside me as we crossed the last two hundred yards and began to walk up the driveway toward the house.

I knew Mom would be inside, and I could only hope she was too busy to look out the front windows as we made our way up the hundred-foot-long graveled drive. The cloud cover seemed to brighten slightly as we neared the house, and that was just enough of a distraction to keep me from noticing the sudden shimmer next to the big oak tree beside the driveway.

I wouldn't have believed that a ghost could gasp, but a sound escaped Sarah that couldn't have been anything else. I looked toward her again. Her hands were over her mouth again, as they had been when she first saw me, but her eyes were wide and shining.

I also hadn't thought a ghost could shed visible tears, either, but I was wrong about that, too.

She was staring at the oak, and when I followed her gaze, I saw what had to be my uncle, but his face was almost unrecognizable. He looked younger, and the decades of bitterness and nastiness were gone from his expression. He looked so much like me that it was scary.

He was smiling back at her too, and then his mouth opened, and for the first time in my life, I heard him laugh. It was a pleasant sound, but windy, and seeming to come from a distance. He wasn't as brilliant as Sarah, either, but when I looked back at her, I saw that she had grown dimmer.

I was confused for a moment, but then I remembered Tommy, and how the cloud cover had brightened when we arrived. The treeline was closer at the farm than at New Jerusalem, but just above it, behind the low rainclouds, I could see a bright patch that could only be one thing.

Sarah had left my side. I looked back just in time to see her leap into Fred's arms, and he spun her effortlessly around several times, their eyes locked on each other. Then he clasped her to himself, and for almost a minute, they didn't move at all. Out of the corner of my eye, I could see the sky steadily clearing in one spot.

Finally, he let her down – I wondered whether he could feel her weight – and they both turned to look at me, beaming with identical smiles. My own grin must have been at least as wide. Fred looked as though he had never had a bad day in his life, but it was Sarah's face that took my breath away. I didn't realize until that moment how heavily the burden of half a century of waiting had weighed upon her.

But I knew it was time, and though I didn't want to say goodbye, they had waited long enough. I looked at Sarah, and as I pointed to the blazing portal in the sky where the clouds had parted, I could barely whisper: "Remember Tommy?"

She gave that odd gasp again, and when she saw where I was pointing, the tears came again. Fred laughed once more, and they embraced again; then they broke apart, and clasping each other's hands, they began to walk toward their final destination, ascending as they receded.

The light hurt my eyes, but I still tried to watch them, and at the last moment, Fred glanced back toward me. He waved, and I waved back, and I heard a faint call from him as they faded out: "Steven, dig between the two big roots of that oak tree. Keep what you find. Consider it your inheritance from your favorite uncle."

"Thank you!" I tried to shout back, but the words died in whispers on my lips as they disappeared in the air, and the light in the sky faded.

CHAPTER EIGHT

I ENDED UP SPENDING three days at home after that.

No, I wasn't suspended from school, and I wasn't grounded, though my mom was pretty unhappy with me coming back to the house. I had planned on calling Chad to take me to get my truck, but by that afternoon, I knew I was coming down with a serious cold. For the two days that followed, I was in bed most of the time.

I let my dad know where I left the truck, and told him that it had broken down at the park before school. He and my mom went to get it that evening, and though he commented that it started fine when he tried it, he didn't question me any further. Mom, on the other hand, suspected something was up, and though she didn't say anything while I was sick, I knew sooner or later the reckoning would come.

When I got to school on Thursday, Chad and Stephanie were waiting with Lori and Joey beside Joey's truck. I knew they'd be there – I had talked with Chad for a few minutes while my parents were getting the truck, but had only been able to tell him a little of what had happened before I had to go back to bed. Stephanie especially looked tense and expectant as I approached them.

I got right to the point. "Sarah's gone home," I said, looking straight at Stephanie. "We walked all the way back to the farm. Uncle Fred was waiting for her. He hadn't appeared before then."

"Was it like what happened with Tommy?" Chad asked. Lori and Joey didn't speak, but they were watching us attentively.

"It was exactly like that," I answered. "I think Fred was waiting for her there because it was where her home should have been. He didn't look the same, either," I added. "I'd never seen him smile before. He looked like he'd just gotten home from the army, back in 1953. He almost looked like one of us."

I related the entire story of our journey as quickly as I could, knowing we would have to get to class in a few minutes. I was describing how the window in the sky had appeared, and how they had been walking toward it, when I stopped. I had forgotten Fred's last words to me until then, and I wasn't sure I wanted to let slip what he had told me.

Stephanie didn't notice. "And they just disappeared? Like Tommy?" she asked. I nodded in reply, looking at each of them in turn.

"The thing is, every one of those ghosts at First New Jerusalem are waiting to go home. Some of them might not even know it, but they are." I sighed. "I probably won't be living here very long, since we're moving as soon as my dad sells the farm, but you guys will all be here next year. Maybe you can help more of them get out of that graveyard."

Stephanie bit her lip. "I don't know. We've found out a lot about some of them, but most of them don't even notice us. How are we supposed to help them?"

"It might not just be you guys," I answered. "There'll be new kids here every school year. Maybe you can recruit a few of them, and make it like a secret society. There's probably a few people in town that could help, too. I'd bet that librarian knows something's up with that cemetery, at least. She might not want to admit it. Ms. Mollie and Ambrose might know something, too. And they can't be the only ones."

"So you're saying we should start a school club? The Ghost Club?" Joey looked skeptical.

"I'd bet you could get one of the Civics teachers to sponsor it. It wouldn't be an actual Ghost Club – more like a Junior Historical Society, or something like that. On the outside, it'd just look like any other service club," I said. "But it'd be great for finding the sort of kids who'd be really interested in what you're doing. Most of the school club members wouldn't need to know about the ghosts – that'd be the secret part."

Chad thought about that. "I guess that could work, but how would that make us different from 4-H or Junior Civitan or the Key Club?"

"Those are active service organizations," Stephanie answered. I could see that she was beginning to warm to the idea. "We'd be more of a historical group. There'd be enough to do, too. There's a lot of ghosts that need our help."

We all became quiet, each of us thinking over the idea, until the warning bell for class sounded. I looked around at each of my friends as we began making our way toward the building.

THAT AFTERNOON, AS I drove back to the farm, I thought about what I would tell my parents. Obviously, I couldn't tell them the entire story, but the historical club idea gave me some cover. I knew I would have to tell them the story about Sarah and Fred, though.

I was so engrossed in thinking about how I would broach the subject that I didn't notice that my dad had come home until I was about to turn into the driveway. He had just gotten out of his car and was watching me make the turn off the road onto the gravel. I brought the truck alongside the car and stopped a few feet from the big oak tree. Just before I unfastened the seatbelt, I noticed the two big roots Fred had mentioned, and made a note to myself to dig there before sunset.

I was expecting to be in trouble, given how the first half of the week had gone, but the grin on Dad's face caught me off guard. I hopped out of the truck, trying not to look puzzled. "Hi, Dad," I said.

"Hi, son. Ready to move back to Tuckerton after the school year ends?" he asked in reply.

That could only have meant one thing. "Oh, man! Someone bought this place?" I asked, hoping I wasn't going to be disappointed.

"Yep!" he answered, clearly as pleased as I felt. "Got almost what I wanted for it. The buyer wants to subdivide it and build a new neighborhood here."

"Really? All the way out here?" I asked. "Isn't it a bit far?"

"Not really," Dad answered. "There's three or four more big plots that've sold this year." He paused thoughtfully. "It seems like this place is finally starting to change. In ten years, the farms will all be gone."

"Wow." I was so surprised to hear this that I forgot about Fred and Sarah for a moment. "I just don't understand why anyone would ever want to move here."

Dad laughed at that. "Me either, to tell you the truth. I don't know if even your uncle liked it here."

I hesitated for a second, but instinctively, I knew it was time to tell him. "I'm pretty sure he didn't. I found an old box of his when I cleared out the attic. Did you know he was supposed to get married when he came back from Korea?"

His smile froze on his face, and then faded. His eyes were disbelieving. "Married? *Fred*?" he asked incredulously.

"Yeah," I answered. "There was a girl who lived here. Her name was Sarah Beckwith. He met her before he went to Korea, and was going to marry her when he came back. I'll tell you the story when we get inside."

I went past him, heading up the steps onto the porch, and then into the house. I don't think he moved for five minutes. I know it took him longer than that to come in, because I was on our sofa waiting for him when he finally came through the door.

He sat on the other end of the sofa, looking at the TV without really watching it – staring, really. I could tell he'd never heard anything about Sarah. I thought that was a shame.

"You found a box in the attic," he finally said.

"Yeah," I answered. "When I saw what was in it, I went through the rest of the stuff up there. Most of it was trash, but I found some receipts from the local florist. He put flowers on her grave every month for over twenty years."

"Wait. Her *grave*?" Dad asked. "What happened to this girl?"

It took me nearly twenty minutes to tell the entire story, all the while being careful not to mention the ghosts. I wasn't sure he was ready to know about them – I didn't know if he'd ever be ready – and since we would be leaving soon anyway, I thought it would be best to leave them out of it. I had plenty of evidence of what had happened without them, anyway.

Dad actually let me tell him everything without interrupting even once. I don't know if he was so surprised that he couldn't speak, but I thought he might be. I had to explain that the truck broke down on the morning we went to verify where Sarah was buried.

I didn't realize that Mom had been listening in until she commented, "so that's why you were at the park. I was wondering why you all were meeting there."

I nodded to her. "It was hard to find the plot. It's at the back of the cemetery, and the hedge has grown up around it." Then I looked back at my dad for a second, and then my eyes came to rest on the mantel, where Fred's urn still stood.

"I'd like to place the urn in the Beckwiths' plot," I said. "The family's gone, and it's pretty well hidden. I don't think anyone will mess with it. We can scatter his ashes there, if that's better. But they should be together." I sighed. "I never thought I would feel sorry for him, but I do. He was really in love with Sarah. We found some pictures of her in the old newspaper issues at the library, and believe me, she was *gorgeous*. And popular, too. I wish I'd gotten to meet her when she was alive."

Dad and Mom exchanged an odd look. "I knew something was going on with you," Mom finally observed. That didn't surprise me, but I was glad to have a cover story that didn't involve anything supernatural.

I FINALLY GOT MY chance on Saturday morning. Mom and Dad were sleeping in, so I got up early and went out to the garage. Fred's old, half-rusted spade stood in a corner. We'd knocked the cobwebs off it, but other than that, it hadn't been touched since he died. I hoped it wouldn't break before I could dig up whatever my uncle had left behind.

I went over to the tree, and began digging about a foot away from it, midway between the two large roots Fred had mentioned. The ground was relatively soft, and within a few minutes I had gotten about a foot and a half into the ground when I felt the spade hit something hard.

Hoping it wasn't a rock, I scraped across the bottom of the hole with the shovel, and saw dark metal showing through scratches in the red earth. Working more carefully, I widened the hole until I had found the box's edges. After a few minutes of getting damp, muddy red clay on my hands and under my fingernails, I succeeded in prizing it from the hole.

It was an old metal strongbox with a hinged lock, like an antique version of the cash boxes used in the school lunchroom. When I pulled at the lock, it opened easily. Before I lifted the lid, I took a look around to make sure no one was watching — which was silly, except that I knew I'd have all kinds of trouble trying to explain what I was doing to Mom and Dad. No one was in sight, so I carried it carefully into the old garage, and placed it on Fred's dingy old work table.

I stared at it for a few minutes, wondering what could be inside it. I hoped I wasn't building up anticipation over nothing, but I was pretty sure there was something important inside. I didn't think Fred would have told me about it, just as he was leaving forever, if it was nothing.

Or maybe he would have. Fred and I had never liked each other – maybe because of the family resemblance, and maybe because I reminded him of when he was young, and of the rotten fate that had taken Sarah away from him. Still, I had been able to figure it all out, and brought them back together. So he probably hadn't done it as a trick or out of meanness.

There was only one way I would find out. Taking a deep breath, I lifted the lid. For a moment, I was confused by what I saw; I thought it contained a plastic bag full of large spools of ribbon. Then I realized that the round objects were actually rolls of money, each bound by a rubber band, and the whole lot contained in a freezer bag. There were twelve of them in there. My heart skipped a beat when I realized that the outside bill on each roll was a hundred-dollar bill.

After hastily wiping my hands on my jeans, I lifted the bag out, opened it, and extracted one of the rolls. My hands were shaking so badly that I could barely get the rubber band off. It took me almost a full minute to align the money together and count it; the roll contained fifty bills, and every single one had Benjamin Franklin on the front.

Holey socks. Five thousand dollars, times twelve rolls. *Sixty thousand dollars!*

I was already stuffing the money back in the bag, my mind racing, when I saw a folded sheet of notebook paper in the bottom of the box. It had been tucked underneath the money, and for obvious reasons, I hadn't noticed it.   Taking it out of the box, I unfolded it and read:

TO MY NEPHEW, STEVEN –

The contents of this box are the accumulated takings of my time working to destroy Bill Beckwith's operation. I succeeded, but in this town, there are no final victories, and in the end, nothing really changed here.

The one thing I desired most has been lost to me, and I do not know as I write whether there will ever be a restoration. I leave this here, in hope that you will find our story amidst my effects after I have passed on. If I am granted the chance to remain and wait for Sarah, I will wait here.

If you find this, Steven, it will mean you have learned one of the most important secrets of this awful town, and that you have brought my beloved Sarah to me. For that, I can never thank you enough.

Please accept this gift in token of my gratitude, and promise me that you will leave McDowell Mills at your first opportunity – and that you will never come back.

Also, please tell your parents to place my remains in the Beckwith plot. If you need to tell them the whole story, feel free to do so. Perhaps that will help them understand what happened.

And if anyone else should find this box, I hope that you will be as cursed by its contents in your lifetime as I was in mine.

- FREDERICK STEVEN SMITH

October 19, 1992

I read the entire note three times, staggered by its contents. I knew he had known about the ghosts – Sarah had told me – but somehow, he had been able to learn the rest of what we had figured out. And my idea of placing the urn with the Beckwiths was obviously in line with his wishes.

I took a deep breath, replaced everything in the box, and took it inside. I had a feeling I was going to be having a long talk with my parents about my future plans.

SEVERAL HOURS LATER, I was sitting in the living room with my dad when the phone rang.

"Steven, it's for you," floated my mom's voice from the kitchen. As I got up to get the phone, Dad glanced over at me. "You might want to keep that business about the money to yourself, son," he cautioned.

I nodded, and went to take the receiver from Mom. "Hello?"

"Hi, Steve." It was Stephanie.

"Hi," I answered, a bit guardedly. I felt bad about that, since she and I shared one of the biggest secrets in the town, but I thought my dad might be right. Besides, he could probably hear me from where he was sitting. It didn't matter, though, because Stephanie got right to the point.

"Steve, there's a rumor going around that your dad sold Fred's farm. Is it true?" she asked.

I sighed. "Yeah," I answered. "I'm going to finish the year here, and then we're moving back."

"Aw," she groaned. "We were hoping you'd be staying here. At least until the end of next year."

"Well, I won't be far away," I answered. "Tuckerton's only about an hour drive, and I have a truck now. I'll definitely be coming back to see you guys."

"Good." I could hear the relief in her voice. "We're going to hunt some more of the ghosts, and see if we can help them find their way home."

"Some of them will want to go," I said. "But remember how the older – older ones would try to keep the newer ones in their place? Some of them might resist. I don't know if they could hurt you, but it might not be the safest thing to be doing." I glanced around, but my mom had left the kitchen. That was a relief. I had come very close to saying "ghosts," along with what I'd said about safety, and that would have started a whole new discussion.

"Chad said something like that," she replied. "But we think that once we start helping them, and the others notice what's going on, they'll start to come around."

I wasn't so sure about that, but it was going to be their project now. "Maybe," I answered her, noncommittally.

"You'd better help, too," she said, more emphatically than I expected. "You're part of this – the biggest part, now. No one else has gotten any of the ghosts home. You did it twice."

Her tone struck me as odd, and I couldn't understand why, until the next sentence tumbled out of her mouth. I think it surprised her as much as it did me.

"Besides, it's just more fun being with you." That one hung in the line between us. I didn't quite know what to say to that, and I knew that even though she hadn't meant to put it that way, it was out there now. I also knew that I couldn't leave her hanging.

It wasn't like I had any girlfriends, I reasoned quickly. None in Tuckerton. None in this crummy town.

Why not? I thought to myself.

"Would you like to go on a date sometime – just the two of us?" I asked. And then I held my breath. If I'd misread this one, it was going to be awkward.

"*Yes,*" she answered. She sounded like she had been spared a punishment. "Soon."

This might be okay, I thought, until one more thing occurred to me. "What about Chad?"

"Chad and I dated last year," Stephanie replied. "We went out a few times before we decided we were better off as friends. He knows I like you."

I had to laugh a little. "Well, let him know I like you too. And I promise I'll visit as often as I can." I hesitated for an instant. "But you, and the rest of the group, are the only reasons I would ever come back here. I'd like to help you guys find out more about what's going on."

"Good," Stephanie said. I could tell she was really pleased, and I felt good knowing I was the reason. "Look, I have to go. See you Monday?"

"Sure thing," I answered. "Bye."

There was just a moment's pause. "Bye, sweetie," she said, and the line clicked dead.

I stared at the receiver for a few seconds. I was grinning. I couldn't help that. But I took a deep breath, hung the phone up, and went back into the living room. Like Fred, I had found something here I wanted, and like him, even after I left, even with all the warnings to stay away, I knew I'd be coming back.

EPILOGUE

WE MOVED BACK TO Tuckerton five weeks later, the week after school ended. Mom and Dad were able to close on a house just a few blocks from our old one, in a neighborhood I knew well. I was glad to be back, but it wasn't quite the same anymore. I felt like I was putting on a pair of old shoes months after getting a new pair and breaking them in – it was a fit, and it wasn't uncomfortable, but I had gotten used to something else.

Stephanie and I started dating the Friday after Dad told me we'd be moving. We saw each other more and more during the last few weeks of school, but it was still a bit uncertain and awkward, especially since most of the time, our friends would come along on dates. Lori and Joey were still a couple, and Chad would sometimes bring a date, and there were two or three others that would turn up wherever we went. We almost never had a moment alone.

It started to get a bit tense, really. We finally went to the bowling alley – the one the greasers supposedly ran, over in Jackson Creek – and there wasn't any trouble. I guess there were enough of us paying that they thought it would be worthwhile to let us bowl – that, or maybe it was just safety in numbers.

When we got there, I had already decided it was time to make a move. When no one was paying attention, I whispered quickly to Stephanie, "wait a few moments, and then follow me out." She looked puzzled, but I stood up anyway and said aloud, "Shoot. I'll be right back. I left my wallet in the truck." Before anyone could answer, I got up and headed for the glass door.

Once outside, I waited beside the door, a little away from it so as to stay out of sight. Stephanie came out about a minute later, and looked at me quizzically. "What's going on?" she asked me.

"This," I answered. Before she could react, I hugged her, and as I loosened my hold a few seconds later, she pressed her lips to mine. My response was equally enthusiastic, and for several minutes we kind of forgot everything else.

When we finally broke, she looked at me with shining eyes. "Finally!" she breathed.

I smiled, and she began to laugh. "Come on, we can't make them wait on us," she said, and grabbing my hand, she half-dragged me back in. I was still a little dazed. The whole thing had gone much better than I had dared to hope.

When we got back to our lane and I began to change into my rented shoes, I heard Chad clear his throat and say, in a voice that would have done Mr. Singer proud – most of the building's occupants obviously heard him – "so. You finally kiss her?"

I knew my expression had already given me away, but I couldn't stop the grin from blooming on my reddening face. Our friends started applauding. So did about half the people in the bowling alley.

So much for secrecy. "Was it really that obvious?" I asked.

"Well, the wallet bulging out of your back pocket as you walked off was sort of a giveaway," Lori observed.

"Very smooth," Joey added.

I looked over at Stephanie, and though she looked as embarrassed as myself, I knew she cared as little as I did. After all, we *were* among friends.

"Screw it," I mumbled, and moved over to sit next to her. She hugged me again, and a few catcalls sounded from the lanes near us.

"Okay, okay, enough. Let's bowl," Chad said.

THREE DAYS AFTER I returned to school, the three of us had gone to the library, and related the events of that past week – at least, an edited version of them – to Miss Roberts, as we had promised we would.

She had listened attentively as we related the story Mollie had told us, and looked visibly shaken when she learned the truth of Sarah's death. When we finished, she looked drained, and yet relieved.

Her expression toward me had changed as well, and when she had thanked us for having told the entire story, we started to leave – but she called after us, so that we stopped and looked back toward her.

She studied us for some time, one by one, but her eyes rested on me last. She seemed to be trying to say something, but no words were coming. I finally broke the silence.

"Miss Roberts, I know I promised I would leave and never come back, but I think this place may finally be beginning to change. People are starting to move in here. My uncle's farm is going to be turned into a subdivision, and my dad thinks that in ten years, the farms will all be gone.

"I'm moving back to Tuckerton, but I'm going to come visit as often as I can." I glanced toward Stephanie, and she smiled back at me. "I think part of making things change here is facing what has been going on for so long, and resolving all these – these old stories."

I wasn't sure how she would respond, and it looked like she wasn't sure herself. We looked at each other for almost fifteen seconds before she finally said, "I do hope you're right," and favored me with an actual smile. I was almost too surprised to smile back.

We turned again to leave, and as we reached the exit, her voice floated over the shelves to us: "Come back whenever you need help finding the truth of these old stories."

I glanced back, but all I saw was the door of her office as it closed.

STEPHANIE AND I continued to date after I returned to Tuckerton, and spoke to each other over the phone almost every day over the summer. I took a job on the local mall staff, cleaning up the place in the evenings and relining the parking lot and doing maintenance during the day. It paid reasonably well and there were plenty of work hours – not that I really needed the money, other than for hanging out with my friends.

The rest of the gang back in McDowell Mills had started searching the town records for all of the ghosts they could identify, hoping to duplicate what we'd accomplished with Sarah and Tommy. For most of the summer they didn't find much, but about a week before school started, I got a call from Stephanie. As soon as I took the phone from my mom, she spoke without preamble.

"We found Mr. Abbott's wife," she said. "Chad and I are going to visit her."

"Really?" I replied in surprise. "How'd you manage that?"

"It's a long story and most of it was really boring, but we were able to find out where she moved by tracing Mr. Abbott's sister. She went to Tuccoa Falls, up near Lake Hartwell, and once we found that out, we wrote to her and found where his wife went. Her name is Helena, and she lives in a nursing home in Lavonia. We're going to go up there next Saturday. Want to come?"

It actually sounded interesting, even though I'd been through the area near Lavonia, and it was so backward that it made McDowell Mills seem like Las Vegas by comparison. "Sure. Let me know when you're leaving."

"We figured you could meet us here, and then we could take the state highway up through Athens. It's almost a three-hour drive." She hesitated. "I hope they let us talk to her. I don't know why she's in a nursing home."

I shrugged. "Usually, people in nursing homes *want* visitors. A lot of people park their old relatives there and forget them. I doubt it'll be that difficult." I paused, remembering something I'd heard years ago, at Christmas, when our elementary school chorus had gone to sing in a similar facility.

"Bring a lot of boxes of tissues, for the people there. They're always running short."

"Good idea. I'll let you know when we're meeting." Stephanie paused, and then blurted, "I love you."

She'd never said that before, but I knew the right answer. "I love you, too, Steph," I answered. And I meant it.

"We can seal that with a kiss on Saturday," she said. "I can't wait to see you again."

Sometimes during the summer, I had regretted the amount of work I was getting. This was definitely one of those times – the more so since, thanks to Fred, I no longer needed to save so much for college. Still, she didn't know that. I hadn't told anyone about the money. Besides, if I was able to maintain my grades and get a scholarship, that would be more left over for me afterwards.

"I can't wait, either. Talk with you tomorrow?" I asked.

"Okay. Love you bye," she said in a rush, and hung up before I could reply.

I hung up the phone, and took a deep breath. Senior year hadn't started quite yet, but it already promised to be interesting in a lot of different ways.

ABOUT THE AUTHOR

M.C. VAUGHN is a retired industrial engineering generalist, a native Atlantan and a longtime resident of a south-metro-Atlanta county that bears a strong resemblance to the setting of this novel. When not writing or editing, he is an avid baseball fan and historian, and a solid (though singularly unlucky) poker player.

Salem's Ghosts is his fourth novel and the first in this series. He now lives with his family in the Savannah, Ga. area.

www.ingramcontent.com/pod-product-compliance
Lightning Source LLC
Chambersburg PA
CBHW070405200726
48294CB00003B/1090